Blood Runs Through The Heart

L.L. Shelton

T.A. Williams

Blood Runs Through The Heart

Blood Runs Through The Heart
is a work of fiction. Names, characters, places, and incidents are the products of the author's imagination or are used fictitiously. Any resemblance to actual events, locales, or persons, living or dead, is entirely coincidental.

Published by: L.L. Shelton
Newport News, Virginia
ISBN: 9781702652490
First Edition

Chapters

Blood Runs Through The Heart

Dedicated to

My sister

Patsy Ann Shelton Allen

On her 71st Birthday

Without whose support, enthusiasm, and love, this story might still be untold. You cheered me to new heights and consoled me when I have fallen. You embraced me with open arms and never turned away. My family, my sister, my friend, and my heart.

Forever bonded by the blood that runs through our hearts.

All my love for eternity.

Your little sister

Angel (L.L. Shelton)

Blood Runs Through The Heart

1

She-Wolves

The sun is moments from dipping below the horizon. Dark and white fluffy clouds filled the skies as a mixture of colors converged into one canvas. A little nippy this evening, an unusual chill lingered across the skin but never reached the bones. The streets were busy for a Thursday night. Delicious smells from various vendor carts filled the night air while humans, she-wolves, and only a few vampires who tolerated low sun strolled down the brick sidewalks. It was a peaceful world where everyone lived as one. A thought not even possible fifty years ago. Not until the leaders of the three races signed the famous Truths Treaty.

The limo arrived promptly at six in front of the

high-rise apartment complex. The driver, a young blonde girl fresh out of college, stepped from the driver's seat. She was wearing all black that accented the long, curly blonde hair lying on her shoulders. Avoiding eye contact with the passersby, she stood patiently by the limo door, waiting to meet the high-ranking leader of the she-wolves. Not knowing what to expect, her nerves were on high alert. She studied Lady Rochelle's history in college, but now it is about to become a face-to-face reality.

Lady Rochelle rose to power fast in the pack. Fresh out of college, she conquered the high seat within five years. Leading her pack into success, the members of the she-wolves reached all corners of the world. Over a million strong, her wolves remained loyal and trustworthy. Believing in her leadership, they trusted her.

The door flew open, causing the young girl to stand up straight. All the thoughts in her head could not have described the first sight of Lady Rochelle. Legs went on forever; broad shoulders squared as she walked. Muscle tone of her arms and legs enhanced by tight black leather painted her body. Her hair, white as snow, hinted of what was once black. Mystery surrounded her. As she approached, air became still.

Merely inches from her, Lady Rochelle stood. The limo door opened, and the young girl lowered her head in respect. “Close the door.” The raspy voice demanded. The door slammed shut. Lady Rochelle stepped closer, her nose inches from the blonde hair. She sniffed as she walked around, her eyes scanning the toned body. She sniffed again. Long nails scraped down the young girl’s arm, causing her to coward down. Her shoulders lowered, and she bent slightly at the knees and waist with a wobble.

“I smell fear,” Lady Rochelle announced. A low growl emerged from her throat before she spoke again. “Are you scared?” She asked the trembling girl.

“Yes. Yes, ma’am.” The young girl answered, a stutter in her voice.

“You fear me?”

“I am scared that I will disappoint you, Lady.”

“Open the door.” The demand rang out in the night, followed by the second one. “Get in the back of the limo.” Lady Rochelle ordered.

The young girl stood stunned before climbing into the back seat. Her heart was pounding against the rib cage. Blood rushed through her veins from the unexpected request. She was there to drive, instead of joining her in the backseat. She lowered her eyes as she felt her presence in the back seat.

“Lift your eyes to me.” The raspy voice ordered. Her eyes lifted to find dark ones. “Your eyes are beautiful. They are golden. You are gorgeous. What is your name, young one?"

A lump formed in her throat. She swallowed a few times, trying to push it down. "Brandy Lee, my Lady."

"Very nice. A beautiful name, and one of my favorite drinks." Lady Rochelle laid her hand on Brandy Lee's thigh. She watched as a shy smile came across Brandy Lee's lips. "And a sweet smile. Come here. Let me smell you closer."

Brandy Lee scooted an inch as impatient arms pulled her closer, their bodies adjoining. A soft touch pulled blonde strands from the neck, and Brandy Lee felt a breath roll over her skin. She growled, which only fired Lady Rochelle to nibble at the flesh. Lips traced down, kissing lower before tracing back up into the crook of the neck. Lady Rochelle wrapped her fingers around this sexy creature's throat. She squeezed, allowing her nails to dig into the flesh. The blood dripped slowly down; Lady Rochelle pulled back. The unusual smell caused her breath to hitch. Her dark eyes widened.

"You are a virgin?" Lady Rochelle asked with interest.

Brandy lowered her eyes. Shame? Embarrassment?

"Lift those beautiful eyes." The ordered came in a lower tone, followed by a low growl that emerged from deep in the back of her throat. “I will not tolerate shame or fear from my Pack.” Lady Rochelle laid back in the seat, looking out in the window in thought. “So, what’s your answer to my question?

“Yes, ma’am. I am a virgin.”

Lady Rochelle's eyes remained focused out the window. Anticipation made Brandy Lee wiggle in her seat. Had she failed her first job detail? Lady Rochelle broke the uncomfortable silence. “That’s not what concerns me about your smell, even though I can’t understand why such a gorgeous she-wolf is a virgin. No, that is a matter of detail.” She turned her face towards Brandy Lee. “Your blood smells of royalty. Who are you related to?”

Remembering not to lower her eyes, Brandy Lee stiffens in her seat. Her golden eyes gazed into the dark eyes. “I would not know, my Lady. I was in an orphanage during my human stage. I do not know who I am. I was given up as a baby.”

“Hmm . . . Interesting . . . ” Lady Rochelle handed Brandy Lee a tissue. “Clean yourself up. Swallow that fear. I don’t want to smell fear on my driver. Understood? That is one thing that disappoints me. Now exit and drive me to The Redblood Estate.”

Brandy looked at her like she had spoken a foreign language. Seriously? Family or not. Why would she put herself in such a situation? With only her by her side, there was not enough protection. They could kill Lady Rochelle within minutes of arriving.

"Is there a problem, Brandy Lee?" she asked.

"That is the house of the vampires. You have no protection, except for me. I was top in my field in combat studies in college, but we are talking about an army of vampires. I may lose a fight, or worse, fail you."

"There you go again. Afraid of disappointing me. I am sure teachers made you study the history of she-wolves, vampires, and humans in school?"

"Yes, my Lady. I know the queen of the vampires is your sister. Even being related to Queen Lana, you are still in danger. I hope that I have not spoken out of place. Your safety is my main priority."

"Well, thank you for your concern. I will be fine and so will you. Now, take me to Redblood."

2

Vampires

The Redblood Estate, founded in the 18th century by Queen Julia, housed the highest members of vampires. Queen Lana was the successor after Queen Julia perished in a battle over grounds with the she-wolves. After taking the throne, it was her mission for world peace between vampires, she-wolves, and humans. Nearly twenty-five years later, the mission finally accomplished when her sister Rochelle became a leader of the she-wolves.

Queen Lana laid in her chaise lounge with fresh night air whisking over her gown. The material lifted with each gust of the night wind. Her eyes the color of onyx searched the skyline as the day turned to night. Lights glowed in the distance like a smoldering heat. Her luxurious black hair cascaded down her curves, blanketing her.

The knock on the door jarred her from the thoughts, yanking her back into reality. “Enter,” She yelled.

Raven, Queen Lana’s assistant, entered with a push of the door. The silver tray carried the glass of blood. Dressed in an emerald long dress that clung to her body, she glided over the tiles. Reaching her queen, she lowered to her knees. “Your early nightcap, my queen,” Raven said.

“Thank you, Raven. Please, join me.” Lana motioned with her hand for Raven to join her on the lounge chair. “So, is there any news to report?” She asked. The rim lifted to her lips slowly, and the red fluid slipped over her lips. Not waiting to hear Raven’s answer, a soft moan of pleasure released. “Mmmm. An exquisite flavor.” With a slight tilt of her hand, Queen Lana finished half the glass. A long index finger wiped the corner of her mouth before she sucked gently on the tip. “Enjoy,” Lana passed the half-full glass to Raven.

Raven slipped her fingers around the thick glass, pulling it to her mouth, and ravished the sweet taste. Her tongue rolled over her lips. “Delicious,” she murmured before sitting the glass to the side. “My queen, you seem distracted tonight. Is there something bothering you?”

Lana released a long sigh that echoed off the

walls.

"You can trust me," Raven said.

"I know you are trustworthy. Something is off. I can't put my finger on it." Lana responded.

"I can sense it," Raven confirmed. "I think the others sense it too. Talk of an uprising has been roaming around the house."

Lana cocked her head to one side, then back to the other. "Okay, you have my attention. Why haven't you told me about this news?"

"My queen, I just heard of it today."

"Go ahead. I am listening," A hiss followed Lana's last word. She felt her temper rising. She bit down on her lower lip to control the anger. Even though Lana strived for world peace, she had a terrible temper. One that needed to remain caged or it is deadly.

Raven took in air. She ran her fingers through her long brown hair before twisting it in a long rope of strains. She slipped it over her shoulder, allowing the twine of hair to lay softly down her front. The reflection of the half-moon danced in her pupils, along with fear. The last thing she wanted was to be at the end of Queen Lana's wrath.

"I was down by the stables when I heard voices. The feed machinery muffled the women speaking, but I finally identified the two women; Gayle and Betsy. They mentioned something new is stirring amongst the villages; a change is coming. The vampires sense that the she-wolves have a secret that they are hiding. Suddenly, a muffled voice interrupted the conversation between the two."

Raven watched as Lana's eyes squinted in thought, her tongue rolling over her lips. "My sister would have called if she thought there was anything out of the ordinary in her pack. I want to talk to Gayle and Betsy."

A guard's entrance startled Raven, whose nerves were on edge. She jumped up between Queen Lana and the intruder, but relaxed when the older vampire entered. Raven stepped closer. "What is it?" she asked.

"I am sorry to disturb the queen, but her sister Rochelle has arrived." The older vampire stopped halfway and waited for her instructions.

"Allow her entrance." Queen Lana's voice announced from behind Raven. The older vampire nodded her head, retreating from the room.

The door opened, and Raven watched two women walk in. Lady Rochelle led the way, followed by a young girl Raven had never seen. Her eyes studied her as she crossed the room. Usually, Lady Rochelle commanded a room with her looks, but the blonde behind her was stunning. Breathtaking. A low stir in her stomach caused Raven to shuffle between feet. Raven felt the brush of Queen Lana as she rounded her.

"Evening, sis," Lady Rochelle said.

The nickname sis sounded odd to Raven. She couldn't imagine her queen being a sis or imagine her as a child. There were pictures of the human Lana with long dark hair, olive skin, and darken eyes that aged beyond years.

"We need to talk. Privately." Rochelle continued.

Lana turned her head back towards Raven. "Take my sister's assistant to the dining area." She paused and looked at her sister for a name.

"Brandy Lee," Rochelle said.

"Raven, take Brandy Lee and wait for us to call you."

Raven nodded her head. "Yes, my queen."

Lady Rochelle winked at the young girl. "Go with Raven. It's safe. I will come and get you."

The two sisters watched as Raven and Brandy Lee walked out, and the door closed behind them. They turned to each other with the same black onyx eyes. "We have a problem." The words rang out in unison.

3

Young Ones

The heavy door heavy door closed behind them. Raven stood back, motioning down the hallway. Her arm stretched out, guiding Brandy Lee toward a darkened area where rustic lanterns flickered in a hypnotizing dance against stone walls. Greystones laid above in a towering formation worn and chipped, broken, and many mutilated with claw marks. Shadows mystically swayed in the distance. Stagnant air invaded every breath with mold, lime, and blood.

Brandy Lee joggled her head and blew a puff of air from her nose. She planned to keep quiet and wait for Lady Rochelle to pick her up. She never expected to be in a dark hallway with a vampire, especially one that was so beautiful.

"Is something the matter?" Raven asked.

"No, why do you ask?"

"You are not moving, and that puff of air which came from you was disturbing."

"I am not a fan of walking into unknown dark spaces. The air down here reeks of oldness."

The vampire released a laugh that ricocheted off the walls before being swallowed up by the darkness. "You think our air stinks? Have you smelled yourself?"

Before Brandy Lee could answer the smart-ass remark, her ears perked up, the sound of breathing heard just out of sight. The hair on her neck raised. She inhaled. A low rumble from her vocal cords vibrated through the hallway. Her eyes became the color of crimson. Scanning the pitch-black, she found nothing. The breaths were low, and even with her keen wolf eyesight, Brandy Lee's eyes filled with blackness.

Raven stiffened. Her body tensed, and lips parted, releasing a hiss in response to the sudden demeanor change of her guest. Even in the lowest of light, the sharp white points of fangs shined. The words slid between her lips with authority. "Show yourself." Moments passed, but no one appeared.

In a crouch, Brandy Lee's fingernails started to extend into long, razor-sharp claws. She prepared for a fight. Her head shook from side to side, her breaths rapid. Channeling her thoughts, she tried to divert a full change. Brandy Lee could rip off a vampire's head in a half morph, but with Lady Rochelle down the hall with the Queen of the Vampires, that may not be the best move. A hand touched her shoulder. Her head turned to find the glow of Raven's eyes staring down at her.

"Let me take care of this."

With a backward step, she allowed Raven to step forward. If the situation weren't so dire, she would find humor because a vampire was protecting her. Raven's body blocked her from the hallway. In the hunched position behind Raven, her eyes scanned up the emerald green dress and traveled the long slit that revealed a glimpse of her never-ending legs. Her perfect rounded ass teased her. Her lower back curved inward, leaving the imagination to run wild. *Sheesh! She is a beautiful creature.* The thought was a pleasurable distraction.

Raven's voice rang out again. "Show your face. Who threatens us from the dark?" The flames faded, and darkness engulfed the last speck of light. She took a step just as a blast of air slammed into her body, tumbling her over. Her skin rippled like the water of a stream as the invisible force surged pass.

The chilled wind engulfed Brandy Lee. Blonde hair lifted. Her left shoulder took a hit, causing her upper body to twist with her legs holding sturdy. The skin on her upper arm split open as three long tears of blood poured from the wound. She fell to one knee in a daze. The touch of an arm wrapping around her waist, lifting her with the strength of a thousand men and catching her by surprise. As she got carried through the corridors with lightning speed, a blur of lights streamed through her eyes. She caught a glimpse of Raven's face, which was filled with determination and concentration as they traveled. With a thump, her body slammed onto the bed. A wild shake of the head, and she started the change. The chest pushed out and widened by two folds as her face began to extend into the shape of an animal. Breaths sped up. She growled. Anger filled her eyes.

Raven placed two hands on both shoulders of the half-woman, half-wolf. Eyes met, and Raven whispered. "Take a breath. You're safe; I promise. We're in my room." Breaths slowed. Body shapes returned to human form. Raven watched in awe at the beauty.

"What the fuck was that?" Brandy Lee asked with a lost breath.

"I don't know. It was old magic. Only the elders can make themselves invisible to others." Raven examined the torn jacket. "Let me help you." Pulling Brandy Lee to a sitting position, Raven laid Brandy Lee's head against her chest. A quick removal of the chauffeur's jacket and then the blood-stained white shirt. Brandy Lee remained in her bra. The red liquid dripped down her left arm, steadily flowing. Raven curbed her appetite for the sweetness and her urge to seduce the sexy blonde. "I will not lie. What I am about to do will hurt. I need you to trust me."

Wrapping one arm around the back of the head, she pulled Brandy Lee closer. Breathing was difficult from the crushing grip and the closeness to the beautiful woman. With a place of a hand, she covered the three deep slices as warm liquid washed over her fingers. Raven tilted her head back. Her eyes rolled to the back of her head until only white shined in the dim light. Her eyelids fluttered. An arm grasped at Raven's bicep with a deep animalist scream following as the separated skin started to pull together.

The wails of misery only stopped when the last edge of the cuts connected. Tense muscles relaxed, and Brandy Lee was lowered to the bed, exhausted. The magic performed on her drained all her energy. She couldn't lift her arm, while her head felt as if a thousand pounds were laying atop on it. Helplessness overwhelmed her. Her eyes blinked as she fought against the unknown feelings.

"Let's sit you up slowly." The comforting voice spoke.

Wobbling before gaining her balance, Brandy Lee coughed a few times to relieve the desert that settled in her throat. "Thank you." Her fingers ran over the disappearing scar. "How did you do that?"

"It is part of my gift given to me from the Empress of Vampires. We receive a gift when we graduate from college. We all did. My gift was the power of healing myself and others. You are given a gift as well from the head wolf, or whatever you call the top dog. Are you not?"

Rolled eyes followed a puff of air. Brandy Lee urgently stood off the bed. "That was rude." She bumped pass Raven but stopped in her tracks as a hand grabbed her forearm. A pull and she was twisted back towards Raven.

"I am sorry. That was insensitive. Please forgive me. I have never been around such a beautiful beast." Raven's eyes rolled over the bare stomach and perfect breasts like water over the falls. Muscles so tight they took your breath away. Breasts so firm that one's eyes would be a loss. Lips so full, a kiss absorbed. "Your body is exquisite."

A sudden heat arose from deep inside Brandy Lee's belly. The realization that she stood in black slacks and a lace bra overwhelmed her. She grabbed her shirt, tossing it around her shoulders as she rushed to button up.

Raven's eyes watched with intensity.

"I need to inform Lady Rochelle what happened to me. Things are not right. If they would attack me, I can imagine what attempts will be against her." Brandy Lee buttoned the last button.

"Come on. Let's go back to the chambers and

talk to our leaders." Raven grabbed Brandy Lee's hand, and with a pull, they both stepped toward the door.

4
Old Ones

Pouring herself a glass of blood followed by a glass of wine for her sister, Lana longed for wine; although, alcohol does not affect vampires. Oh, she missed the buzz. Lana sat and motioned for her sister to join her. “Something is not sitting right in our community.” Lana started the conversation.

“I can feel it amongst my Pack.” Rochelle took a long draw off her glass. “How are you holding up?”

“Just tired.” Lana responded.

“You don’t get tired. So, what is wrong?”

“Okay, I am worried. Raven overheard a conversation between two vampires. They’re talking about an uprising. She told me a few minutes before you arrived. It doesn’t sit well with me.”

“Hmmm? Doesn’t sound good.” Rochelle answered before she stood up and walked over to the glass door. It was the time of the night that was the darkness. She could feel movement in every corner of the city. Her Pack was active tonight with howling lingering in the distance. Her eyes scanned the horizon before lowering down to a pathway that led out toward the lake. "Lana. Come here." Rochelle pointed toward an old oak tree; the roots emerging from the ground like crooked fingers. The branches reached down to scoop up anything in the path. Behind the aged bark stood a shadowy figure looking up toward them. A deep black hole replaced a face, while red eyes glowed in the darkness. Lana focused downward with intensity. The hooded creature was mentally blocking her from reading her thoughts. Old Magic. An Elder.

Suddenly, using arms and legs, the creature climbed halfway up the tree before coming to a stop. Its head cocked side to side. With a sudden scurry, the creature pulled itself to the alternate side of the tree. Tilting its head to the left and then slowly to the right, the red eyes peered from the hallows. They grew bright but then dimmed with the rhythm of a heartbeat.

The change went without notice until a snarl rumbled in the night. Lana glanced to the right, finding Rochelle had changed into wolf form. White fur with black specks glowed in the night. Massive muscles curved into perfect shape. Her body leaned back on her hind legs, ready to pounce.

The upper lip curled upward, and saliva glistened off her canine teeth. A growl rattled from her. Rochelle's shoulders met Lana's shoulder in a vast presence. Turning her head for a glance that only lasted seconds, her eyes widened. With a push, she launched off the balcony.

"Noooo!" Lana's scream fell on empty ears. Her face distorted with anger. Her fangs grew out, and fingernails turned to daggers. She leaped into the night using her superpowers. Lana landed on a branch just as Rochelle pounced at the creature.

A raging force of wind swirled the old oak encasing the elder's body. Her body contorted to black smoke, starting at the feet and engulfing the body until only a black mist swirled in the air. Rochelle hit the tree as her body absorbed the floating mixture. A cold chill froze the warm blood that ran through her veins. The breath pushed from her lungs with such force that the night spun in front of her. Consequently, she fell to the ground.

The ground shook as Lana landed on two feet beside her fallen sister. She laid still on her side, her eyes closed. A tongue dangled out between a parted mouth. Lana squatted down next to her, noticing how the stomach raised with each breath.
"Rochelle," Lana placed a hand on her sister's head, stroking the fur. "Open your eyes."

Her heavy eyelids fluttering, Rochelle snapped her powerful jaw. She bit into air. Another bite and teeth crunched into one another. Two more quick ones as she shook her head. When a hand touched her, she leaped up and snapped down towards the touch.

"Damnit, Rochelle. If you bite me, I'll kick your ass, Bitch." Lana stretched out her fingers in an examination. Rochelle had the strength to sever her hand in one chomp.

Rochelle wobbled sideways before shaking the cobwebs loose. After finding her footing, her eyes lowered, followed by her head. She took a few steps, rubbing her nose into her sister's hand. *"I'm sorry."* Her thoughts read by Lana. Rochelle sat back on her behind.

Lana rubbed her head. "That was a dumb ass move. I've told you how powerful our elders are and the old magic they carry. You're lucky that you didn't die." Lana touched her sister's face.

"I'm fine. That damn thing freaked me out. I felt danger, and I knew you felt it too. Can you help me back into your room? Whatever ghostly magic ran through my veins has made me weak."

"Do me a favor and change back to your human form. You're lighter to carry."

She took a step back with her face reaching towards the moon. A howl echoed, and all the hard muscles turned into soft curves. Her fur shortened into the signature long hair. Her arms withdrew, and she stood on two legs. A shake of the head and the gorgeous Rochelle stood in the moonlight.

The young ladies pushed through the door as Lana landed on the balcony with Rochelle in her arms. Surging past Raven, Brandy Lee scooped up Lady Rochelle in her arms. She carried her across the room and lowered her to a chair. “What happened to you?”

“Don’t worry about me.” Rochelle sniffed. “You have bled.”

“Yes, my Lady; I got attacked.”

“Rochelle,” Lana's voice interrupted. The sisters’ eyes connected. The black pupils spoke to each other without words. “That smell-”

“What smell?” Raven asked.

Two sets of eyes pierced through Brandy Lee as quickening heartbeats filled the room. Years have passed since Rochelle and Lana felt fear. Lana laid her hand on Rochelle’s shoulder, and Rochelle brought up her hand, giving it a soft squeeze.

“Brandy Lee,” They both pronounced her name. “Your blood is of royalty. I think we have found the reason behind the uprising.”

5

The Talk

All four women sat around a large wooden table. The younger ones sat while the two sisters whispered amongst themselves. A few nods of the head and hand gestures gave nothing away to the two girls about the conversation. A final whisper of words and the sisters both turned to face Raven and Brandy Lee.

Queen Lana drew in a deep breath with closed eyes. “We need to talk,” Lana spoke. Her eyes opened. “I need the two of you to sit back and listen to Rochelle and me.” Lana placed both arms on the table and intertwined her fingers. Slightly leaning forward, she began the story.

“Many years ago, vampires and she-wolves ruled

when the world was new. The she-wolves was born first, and the vampires came years later. There were many battles for control of the land. Many died. Too many died."

"My Queen, we studied all this in college." Raven announced.

"That is true, but there are parts not taught to our students which only leaders know. So, allow me to finish. We all take on the human form until college graduation. As you also know, all the councils and leaders are present on graduation day. Humans, vampires, and she-wolves come together on that day to add to their families. Even as a leader, I don't know who a vampire is. Rochelle does not know who will join her pack. We take your blood before the ceremony, and a drop gets placed on the Ancient Paper of Reveal. If the paper remains white, you are human. Red represents the blood; so, if it turns red, you are a vampire. Although, you are a she-wolf if your paper is blue. This process is done in private with only one person from each race at the blood's reading." Lana sat back in the chair, allowing the revealed information to sink in with the two women.

"So, we carry the DNA of our race from birth?" Brandy Lee asked.

"Yes, you are born as one of the races, but it remains suppressed in the human form until the day you graduate. That is why you learn the history of all—The House, The Pack, and Human Race." Lana explained.

Rochelle leaned forward toward Raven and Brandy Lee. The two women sat on the edge of their chairs, waiting for the story to continue. Rochelle started. "There are holes in the story of why your blood smells of royalty. What we have come up with is this. The royalty blood running through your veins got revealed at the Ancient Paper ceremony. Any she-wolf or vampire in the room would have smelt the blood. Royalty blood is unique, and only the highest council can detect it." Rochelle waved her hand between her and Lana before pointing at Raven. "That is why Raven isn't noticing the unique aroma coming from Brandy Lee's blood."

Her hands twisted around each other in a nervous habit. Brandy Lee bit at her lower lip. Rochelle reached over and grabbed the young girl's hands, stopping the twirling. A calmness spread throughout her body from the one-touch. "How could I be of the Royal Family? They've been extinct for thousands of years. It makes no sense." Brandy Lee's words escaped with uncertainty.

Lana leaned back forward. "That is one of the holes we have to figure out. We're all born to human women. That woman's reproductive eggs will have the heritage trait the baby will receive. We know that all males are human, so they are not a factor. Only female babies become vampires or she-wolves. But there is another hole. The vampire that was in the room during the Ancient Reveal smelt the blood. And so, she must have reported it to the elders. The question is: why didn't the she-wolf present at the time report it?"

"It was an elder that attacked Brandy Lee earlier." The intensity in Raven's voice rang out.

Lana looked over to her sister. "The same one that was watching us."

"Most definitely." Rochelle acknowledged with a nod. The table got quiet for a moment with all women in thought. Rochelle continued. "So now we need to talk about what's next. Brandy Lee, I am afraid that there has been a hit placed out on you. Yes, and I am afraid the kill order was from my House. The elders want you dead. They are most likely afraid that if you are royalty, the she-wolves will take the world over. The elders are doing this on their own or with council help, but not with mine. The kill order was kept from me because I am Rochelle's sister. It seems as if I have lost control of my vampires." The statement was hurtful, and the confession that she didn't have control of her House was unnerving. The mere thought of any vampires going against her authority made her sick to her stomach.

Lady Rochelle sat straight up. Pulling her phone out, she flipped through the web. "Shit! Where the hell are you?" She mumbled as she flipped through it again.

"Sis?" Lana said but was cut off with a finger held up to her face.

"Here it is." She skimmed the article. "They found one of our council members dead on the night of Brandy Lee's paper reveal and graduation, ruling it an accident. They found her in a river near the ceremony with a blood alcohol level ten times that of the legal limit. Her blood was frozen inside her veins. The news reported it was from the cold water in the river. I believe Lady Prim was the she-wolf at the ceremony, and an elder vampire attacked her. The same cold that chilled my blood earlier killed her."

Brandy Lee looked over at the phone. "That explains why the Pack doesn't know about my blood. The news never got back to the council. Lady Prim died before she delivered it."

Lady Rochelle shook her head up and down in agreement. Queen Lana laid her head on her sister's shoulder. Rochelle pressed her head onto Lana's head. She opened her thoughts to her sister. *It isn't your fault. You are not responsible for a rogue vampire. Brandy Lee needs to get to my high council. Let's tell her the way.* Lana's head moved up and down in agreement. Lady Rochelle grabbed both of Brandy Lee's hands into hers. She inhaled before starting the last part of the talk. This next part was going to either save Brandy Lee or kill her. Either way, the future of the she-wolves was unknown.

"We need to get you to the high council. The seniors are the only ones that will have the answer. You will have to travel to reach them." Rochelle paused. Her eyes met the golden- brown ones before whispering to her. "You have to travel through The Dark Forrest."

Raven spoke louder than she expected. "No one has ever made it through there alive. You can't seriously think she will go alone. My Queen, please stop this." Raven didn't know what had suddenly riled her up. The short time with the beautiful blonde had her insides mixed up.

"I will go with her." Rochelle announced.

"No, my Lady. The Pack can't afford for anything to happen to you. I will go alone."

"No. You will not. I will go with you." The voice rang out from the right. Brandy Lee turned her head. Her eyes met the emerald greens that stared with conviction. "I only need my Queen's permission.

"You know what you ask?" Lana asked.

Never turning her eyes away from Brandy Lee, Raven whispered, "I know, my Queen, but I must. I need to be with her."

Brandy Lee felt a flush rise from her neck into her cheeks. The intensity of Raven's stare stripped her bare. The same flutter low in her belly returned. She lowered her eyes. A cough came from her left, and she lifted her eyes back up. Her leader's words from before rang out in her head. *Do not lower your eyes*.

"Raven, take Brandy Lee to your room, and keep her safe till the sun goes back down. We only have another hour of darkness. It is too late to leave. Bolt your door. Close your vents and windows. We don't need an elder getting in. Rochelle can sleep in here with me. We'll prepare for your travels tomorrow." Queen Lana's words paused. "Our future is about to change."

6
Goodbyes

Sunflowers painted the field bright yellow. Three sides of the grassy area breathed hope and happiness. The fourth represented fear and death with trees twisting and turning around each — the Dark Forest. A pathway was impossible to find in the woodland. From the sturdy trunks, roots reached out and dug into the dirt. Branches swayed. Snakes slithered in and out of darkening holes. The forest dared all to enter with evil and old magic hidden in every corner. Only a few vampires or wolves in the past attempted to travel through the path of hell. The forest protected the two councils on the other side — a haven for the assembly of vampires and she-wolves.

The four women stood amongst the sunflowers hidden from any onlookers' view. They had escaped the estate with a tarp covering Lana and Raven during high sun. Now, the sun laid very low in the distance with pain from the sunrays tolerable.

Queen Lana and Lady Rochelle stepped towards their two younger counterparts. Lana stood in front of Raven. She would never admit it, but the fear that she felt for her assistant was disturbing. Never seeing Raven again was unsettling, because she had grown fond of her. Lana handed the backpack to Raven. Standing tall, she tossed the bag over one shoulder. With her brown hair pulled back into a ponytail, her high cheeks only accented the strong chin. She wore camouflage pants and a green tank top. Boots covered her feet for protection.

"Let's walk." Queen Lana said as she grabbed Raven's hand. They strolled hand in hand. "This journey will not be easy. The forest will try to kill you. It places evil and old magic throughout the woods to protect the councils. Are you sure about this?"

"Yes, my Queen. It's hard to explain, but my inner voice tells me I need to help Brandy Lee make it to the other side and back. I know that I might die."

"Remember, not all that can be trusted can be. Not all that are untrusted are." Lana said.

"I don't understand." Raven said with a tilt of the head.

"You will. I have killed many in my lifetime. You have killed none. I made sure of that when I brought the different worlds together in harmony. We have shielded you. I made you weak."

"I am not weak." Raven went on the defense.

"Not physically, but you are naïve in some ways. If the time comes for you to kill, don't think. Don't hesitate, or they'll kill you. Remember, everything in those woods is there to protect, and you are a threat. Do you have any questions?"

"Will the Council of the House help us?"

Lana pondered for a moment. "I don't know. The council may have ordered the elders to kill Brandy Lee. If that is the case, count on no help. They will be out to kill her and you. Their strength is beyond imaginable; so, enter with caution." Lana watched Raven inhale and exhale. Her body language reeked of nervousness. She was putting up a good front. Lana rubbed her arm before cupping the side of her face. "I have something to give you. Kneel before me." Lana ordered.

Without question, she fell to her knees. The sun faded away, and darkness surrounded them. The wind picked up, and Lana's cape waved in the air. Her long black hair soared upwards. Placing both hands on each side of Raven's face, she closed her eyes. Her body stiffened as her mouth parted. Her fangs grew. Fingernails extended to points. Lana's eyes opened, and solid white eyes replaced the black ones. Lana twisted and swayed her neck like an Egyptian cobra. She fell to the soil inches from

Raven's face. A hiss released into the night. Bringing a long fingernail to her own skin, with a flick, she slit her wrist.

The smell of the Queen's blood ignited Raven's urges. She closed her eyes. Long fingers wrapped around her neck, pulling her forward.

"Feed, my child." Queen Lana ordered.

Raven's fangs sunk into the sweet nectar, and she fed her thirst. Veins tingled as the blood rushed through the heart like a raging river. Her hunger heightened her senses. With both hands, she pulled the bleeding arm hard into her mouth, digging in deeper. Low moans escaped from above her. The blood so thick and sweet that the gratification crashed throughout her body. Raven felt a hand grab her hair and pull her back. Blood dripped from her mouth. Her breath was ragged.

"I'm sorry, my Queen." Raven felt funny. Dizzy. She wobbled.

Lana swiped her hand over her wrist, and the cut healed. Her eyes turned to onyx. She inhaled and released a breath. Once she gathered herself, she pulled Raven into an embrace.

"What's the matter with me?" Raven whispered against Lana's chest. The ground spun, and she felt the wind swirl around her. "I feel intoxicated."

"Through my blood, I gave you a gift. Let it settle inside your blood."

Time passed at a snail's pace before Raven

found her balance. "What gift did you give me?"

"I can't tell you, but when needed, it will reveal itself." Lana stood, lifting Raven with her. "My gift will strengthen you."

"Thank you, my Queen."

Lana nodded. "Come back to me, Raven. I will wait for you. Let's join Rochelle and Brandy Lee. It's time."

Brandy Lee watched as the two other women traveled deeper into the sunflowers. Raven was walking away from her, causing an unexplainable pit in her stomach. It churned with a vengeance. A touch drew her back to the woman that stood in front of her. She smiled a nervous smile but a smile never the least.

"Are you scared?" Rochelle asked.

"I'm sorry. I've failed you again." The young girl whispered.

"It's okay, my child. I'm scared too." Rochelle glanced towards the dense forest. Red eyes glared back from the trees. She ignored the sighting.

"You're afraid of nothing, my Lady." The words grabbed Rochelle's attention back to her companion.

A hand touched the side of the brave one's

cheek. Rochelle looked deep into her eyes. Behind the golden browns lay beauty and determination. "Listen to me. You will face many new challenges in the woods. Trust your instincts. Believe in your heart. You are my Pack, and we are strong. We are one. You'll be a hundred times stronger in your wolf state than your human."

Rochelle walked around Brandy Lee like she did the first time they met. Stopping behind her, she rubbed her face into the shoulder. They remained still. Breaths synchronized. After a long pause, Rochelle lowered Brandy Lee to the ground. They sat cross-legged in front of each other.

"Let's go over a few things. First, don't fear the council. They will welcome you with open arms, but you must allow them to smell your blood. They need to know that you are of the Royal Family. I don't have a clue what will happen after that." Rochelle paused her words. She looked away for a moment.

"Are you okay?" Brandy Lee asked while interweaving their hands together.

"Yes. I was thinking of how your life will be changing. You will have new responsibilities as the Royal Family."

"I just want to drive you around."

Rochelle let out a belly laugh. "I may be driving you, my dear." Reaching into a bag, Rochelle pulled out a few vials of red liquid. Each container was color-coded in green, yellow, and red. She placed them in Brandy Lee's hand. Their hands lingered together with the cold vials between them. "The blood in these vials come from your sisters. You have six, two of each. Each carries power, with red being the strongest. Only use red in a dire emergency. You understand?"

"Yes, I understand. Hopefully, I'll not need to use them." Brandy Lee placed the vials in her backpack. "Thank you, Lady Rochelle. My head is stilling spinning, but I would be lost without you." The words choked out.

"You'll be fine." A finger pointed into the middle of the young she-wolf's chest. " Blood runs through the heart. Lead with this."

The four-women joined back together and stood in a circle. The night was an hour into darkness. With the last few instructions explained, the women said their goodbyes. Brandy Lee and Raven turned on their heels and took the first step together.

7
First Step

Two travelers stood at the edge where the green grass ended and the black moss began, their eyes searching the timber in the hope of a hint or a suggestion that would carry them forward. Nothing but darkness stared back. Emptiness. A shadow crept from under the moss and skimmed the whitetip of Brandy Lee's Converse sneakers before retracting back. A knot grew in the back of their throats. An old owl hooted, which drew attention to the trees. Its big eyes rolled around before its wings spread, taking flight.

Raven reached down and grabbed Brandy Lee's hand. Holding hands would be a romantic gesture, if not for the circumstances. Her heart pounded against her rib cage. With a soft squeeze and a comforting gaze, Raven pulled Brandy Lee across the line into The Dark Forest, leading them down a small path covered in vines and roots. Brandy Lee stumbled a few times, only to catch herself.

"Raven, you can let go of my hand." Brandy Lee announced on the tail end of a stumble recovery. She enjoyed holding the woman's hand, but now she needed both of her hands for balance.

"Oh, sorry." Raven let go. She puffed her cheeks out in a burst of air. Her eye scaled the tall oaks with her body twisting around in a circle. "I bet I can see for miles from up there."

"You can't be serious. It is so high. What if you fall?"

"I am an excellent climber. Just hold my stuff." Raven removed her backpack, handing it over to Brandy Lee. She smiled. When Brandy Lee smiled back at her, the ends of her mouth turned upwards even more. She melted inside. Raven admired the beauty in front of her. Brandy Lee's eyes were toxic.

"Be careful. If you fall, turn into a bat and flap your wings." Brandy Lee said.

"Brandy?" Raven cocked her head sideways while leaving the second part of her name off on purpose. Placing both hands on her hips, she tried to refrain from laughing. Narrowing her eyes, she said, "I don't turn into a bat, and that hurt."

"Oh, I . . ." Brandy Lee's words stumbled like a drunken fool.

"I'm just joking, Brandy Lee. I really can't turn

into a bat, but I'll be careful." Raven nodded, flashing that charming smile. Her neck bent backward as she studied the towering timber. A hand reached out and touched the bark with a gentle stroke. A bend of the knees and she hurled herself upward. Long nails dug into bark for securement with her feet pressed hard against the tree. She inched her way up in a shimmering crawl, slow at first until she got her rhythm.

Standing at the base of the tree, Brandy Lee watched her disappear into the branches. Her eyes remained focused on the branches above until she heard a rustling in the bushes behind her. Pivoting and crouching down, her surroundings monitored. After a few minutes, she concluded that her imagination was playing tricks on her. "Chill out." She spoke the words out loud to herself. Her eye searched upwards but found nothing but falling leaves. She huffed and sat down at the base of the tree. The image of Raven smiling at her sent a flutter through her stomach. *Why do I get this way? She gets out of my sight and I miss her. Am I scared? That can't be it.* She shook her head, trying to clear her thoughts but they returned. *She is*

beautiful. Those emerald eyes, thin lips and her body; so perfect. So sexy.

This time there was no mistake. The bush stirred. Jumping to a squat, Brandy Lee released a slow-rolling growl. More movement. She inched forward, both hands squeezing the dry dirt between her fingers. The branches separated, and Brandy Lee prepared her body and mind to pounce. Time froze. A squirrel darted out from the brush. Brandy Lee exhaled. *Sheesh.* The little fellow stood up on his two back legs and, with a wiggle of the nose, he hurried off. She scanned the area before scooting until her back laid against the tree. She pulled her legs up, wrapping her arms around them. Her chin laid down on her kneecaps. *Where are you, Raven?*

She regretted leaving Brandy Lee alone on the ground from the moment she started the climb. She hated separating from her, but she was hoping to see something useful. A haze churned around the tree like a blanket, making reaching the top slower. The closer she got to the top, an awful sound grew. Blackbirds. Raven hated birds. It was always a joke around the kitchen table. Her name was Raven, yet, one little birdie will put her to her knees. Birds terrified her, except for good fried chicken. She loved fried chicken. Chicken was not a survival food for her; it was self-indulgent. Her body became still. The silhouette of a hundred wings flapping above her head, the short flights between branches, and the long squawks filling the air had Raven paralyzed. *Shit!* She thought.

Her legs straddled a branch with her back against the tree. She watched while thinking of a way to get out of this. She could go back down and tell Brandy Lee there was nothing up there. Avoid the birds altogether. Living with that lie wouldn't come easy. *Shit!* She bit the bottom of her lip in thought. "I'm a vampire, for God's sake. I can get rid of a few birds." Both hands pushed her body up, but she dropped back down upon hearing a noise.

A low growl materialized from the end of the branch. The noise only a few feet away. Raven's emerald eyes glowed in response to the unknown threat. She displayed her teeth before releasing a hiss. Two red eyes glared from the pitch-dark. They grew bigger. Inch by inch, they came closer.

"Fuck." Raven balanced herself.

The black panther emerged with solid muscles and shimmering black fur, its upper lip raised in anger. The large paws took one step at a time, with each step balletic in its own. Stopping only a jump away from Raven, she raised her head towards the fluttering of birds. With one tremendous leap, she landed on the branch above. Then, she circled a few times before another jump and another. Raven watched as she swatted at the large blackbirds. She felt a rush of relief as the massive cat found the birds more appealing. Her swinging tail in the night was the last image of the panther before she crept away.

Raven laid back against the tree, twisting her fingers around her ponytail. The birds flew away. She needed to look and get back down to Brandy Lee. The thought of her alone set off an alarm. She wouldn't hear cries for help this far up. Reaching the highest branch possible, Raven scanned the horizon. Time was passing, and the sun would rise in four hours. There is a small lake lying in the distance. Raven figured about five miles. If they could make it there before the sun rose, that would be an excellent place to camp for the day. Raven started her decent.

The stirring above her head was the best sound. Raven was coming down. Brandy Lee stood in anticipation. Raven's figure came into sight, and relief washed over her.

When Raven made the last leap to the ground, her neck got wrapped in arms. Trying to play it cool, Raven whispered in her ear, "Did you miss me?"

"Yes, I thought you'd never get back."

"Anything happen while I was gone?" Raven asked.

"No." The response came from the face buried into her shoulder.

"Hey, it's okay. I saw a lake not too far from here." Raven rubbed her back. "Come on. We have to keep moving."

"Okay, sorry." Brandy Lee pulled herself away. She pulled at her t-shirt that had gone sideways and yanked at her cargo shorts. "Let's do this."

Raven smiled and led them deeper into the dark forest.

"Did anything happen up there?" Brandy Lee asked as she followed.

"No, nothing at all. I climbed up and then back down." Raven answered.

8
Five Miles

Raven swatted.

"Damn mosquitos!" Raven fretted. If Brandy Lee heard her, she didn't respond. Raven watched her move ahead through the brushes. The started to widen, which made maneuvering over the stumps and roots easier. They had traveled about two miles so far. Raven didn't want to jinx it, but the trip was going smoothly. Trying to get her mind off things, she admired the sexy ass in front of her. Brandy Lee was hot in her cargo pants. That ass twitching got Raven's heart fluttering. Instead of smacking at the blood-sucking mosquitos, she would love to give that apple ass in front of her a smack. "Damn, that ass is sexy!" Raven's words caught her off guard. *Did I say that out loud? Fuck!*

Brandy Lee swirled her body around, causing

Raven to stop in her tracks before stumbling back. She tripped over the large tree stump, landing on her rear. “Ouch!” Raven screamed out. Brandy Lee towered over her with her hands on both hips. Raven’s eyes traveled the long legs, continuing over her six-pack stomach, past her small breasts, lingering over luscious lips, and finding the golden-brown pupils. *Ut-oh! I am in trouble.* Raven felt those eyes burn a hole through her core.

“Did you say my ass was sexy?”

Raven struggled to get up. She couldn’t figure a way out of this one. It wasn’t the first time her mouth had gotten her in trouble with a woman. She decided the best route would be the honest route. “Sorry, yes; I did. But on my defense, have you seen your ass? It’s quite the distraction.” Then there it was — that smile.

Brandy Lee huffed. “Don’t smile like that at me.” And with a quick turn on her heel, she marched into the woods.

“Wait.” Raven jumped up after her. “Hey, Brandy Lee; stop. Hold on.” With an elbow grab, Raven spun her around. “I’m sorry. Didn’t mean to look at your butt. Just trying to keep my mind off-” She looks around at the scenery. “Our circumstances.” Their bodies inches apart. Only breaths laid between them. “I’m sorry. Forgive me.” Raven said.

Brandy Lee’s head shook, but not in a negative

or an affirmative answer. Closing her eyes, she pinched the bridge of her nose. A headache was forming. "It's okay." She pushed passed her and headed back to the trail. Stopping in her tracks with a half a body turn, she let her words slip out in the dark. "So, you know, that smile of yours is sexy." A quick step, and she moved away.

Raven smiled.

Brandy Lee tossed her backpack on the ground. Two seconds later, Raven tossed hers. They were almost to the lake where they would pitch tents and hold out for the day. Raven was already showing signs of weakness. The sun was on the horizon. Lucky, the thickness of the trees would shelter her for a while. It was time for a short break.

Raven pulled out a bag of blood, gulping it in one breath.

"You okay?" Brandy Lee asked before taking a long draw off her water bottle.

"Yes. Sun will be up in an hour, at the most. Let's sit for a minute to catch our breaths. Then, we will head out to finish the last leg. While we are here, it may be a good idea to talk about our weaknesses and strengths. That way, we know each other."

Agreeing they needed to talk, she pulled two apples from her bag and handed one to Raven. "Okay, where do you want to start?" Brandy said while shining the apple on her shirt.

Such a normal movement has Raven thinking about how sexy she was once again. "You start. Tell me something I need to know about you."

Brandy Lee gathered her thoughts. The first time she caught her breath and could think since leaving the meadow. "Well, as far as my strengths, I am sure you have read them in books. She-wolves don't carry special gifts like vampires do. We all have the same strengths and the same weakness. I'm super strong in my wolf form, but don't underestimate me. I'm strong in human form. My vision is sharp. My jaws are powerful enough to dismember a human or vampire. I have speed, balance, and agility on my side. My claws are sharp enough to take a head off its shoulders in one cut." Brandy Lee inhaled. She continued.

"My weaknesses?" She asked it as a question more than a statement. "Silver can kill me. I heal fast, but I can't heal anyone else like you. Wait. Is that last part a strength? Anyhow, thanks for healing me when the elder cut me; but I could have done it. Plus, it wouldn't have hurt as bad." Brandy Lee twisted the side of her mouth up into a half-smile. She thought it was sweet that Raven was protective over her. "When I change back to my human form, I'm at my most vulnerable. The change drains my strength. I'm hard to kill. It takes chopping my head off."

"You forgot one strength." Raven bent over and whispered in Brandy Lee's ear. "Your sexy ass."

A breath tickled her ear. Brandy Lee turned her head and whispered back. "No, Raven; that's your weakness."

"Touché, Brandy Lee!" Raven thought.

Brandy Lee leaned back on straight arms, propping herself up with both hands. That last remark was out of context for her, but it felt good to catch Raven off guard. Brandy Lee's inner smiled radiated from the small victory. "So, how about you? What do I need to know?"

"My worst enemy is the sun." Raven's eyes raised in search of the ball of fire. A soft glow was in the sky. "It can kill me. A stake in the heart and decapitation will kill me. As far as my strengths, I am fast. Very strong. I have agility. You found out my gift, which is healing myself and others. As we age, we gain gifts. That is why an elder is so gifted. Queen Lana gave me a gift before we left, but she couldn't tell me what it was. So, that's me in a nutshell. Are you ready to go?"

"I have a quick question."

"Shoot." Raven answered.

"If we both are fast, why don't we haul ass to the

other side of the forest?"

"Because. Moving too fast makes us unprotected. The enemy could behead us with ease. Slow is our best defense."

Standing with a palm stretched out, she reached for Brandy Lee. She loved any excuse to touch the girl. Raven got awarded by a smile from the beautiful blonde. Heat rushed straight to Raven's core until the sensation came to a sudden halt. The woman's smile beneath her disappeared.

"I can't move my hands. Something has me pinned." Brandy Lee twisted her mid-section from left to right. Unable to see what had her shackled to the tree, panic started to set in. Closing her eyes and bearing down, she pulled. No movement.

The change started. Brandy Lee's hair began to grow at a rapid rate. Her face extended as it thrashed from side to side. Canine teeth grew. A shiver ran through Raven's body when bones broke and fused back together. Not thinking about the danger, Raven leaned down. She could get bitten or worse. Her hands grabbed each side of Brandy Lee's face.

"Look at me!" Raven watched as the gold eyes focused on her. "I need you to stop. Don't change. Let me see what has you. You will be weak if you change. Just hold on." Raven felt the relaxation overcome Brandy Lee. Raven rubbed the side of her face until she held a human's face. "Thank you.

Now stay still!"

Raven jumped behind to examine the situation. "What the hell?" Raven exclaimed.

"What? What is it?" Brandy Lee twisted her torso again to no avail.

"It looks like a spider web spun around your hands and wrist. When I pull, you pull. Okay? On three. One, two, three!" They gave it their all, but the webbing didn't budge. "Again." They pulled. Not an inch gave. "You didn't feel this wrapping around you?"

"Not at all." Just then, the tiniest spider crawled over her leg. With a swift kick of the leg, it went flying into the middle of the path. Raven had already started to cut at the silky stuff that held Brandy Lee prisoner. The process was slow. "Um…Raven. You need to speed it up."

Raven looked over Brandy Lee's shoulder. Her jaw dropped. She swallowed hard. In a perfect formation, hundreds of tiny spiders stood watching the two women. Raven picked up a branch and tossed it into the middle of them. They retreated and spread out like ripples in water, only to fuse back into formation like magnets. They watched.

Her claws cut faster. Every snip brought Brandy Lee closer to freedom. "Pull with me. Pull, Brandy Lee!" Raven screamed.

Giving it her all, she tugged. The web tore. Her fingers on her left hand wiggled, and then her wrist.

The small accomplishment was short-lived when the army of spiders moved closer. Brandy Lee was only inches away from being swarmed. At that moment, her left hand slipped from the webbing. Raven moved to the right wrist. Without notice, the spiders parted, and the brush rustled in the distance. Brandy Lee's eyes widened. An enormous spider stepped from the shadows with legs five feet tall, a body as big as a car, and a mouth that spread across the head. Huge red eyes stared at the two women.

Brandy Lee panicky searched through her backpack. Pulling the yellow vial of blood from the front pocket, she tossed it back in one swallow. A raging fire ran through her veins. Flipping to her knees, she caught Raven off guard. She watched when Raven's eyes went from narrowed in concentration to large saucers at the sight of the creature. The blood of her sisters ran through Brandy Lee's heart. She pulled until the wood shredded into pieces, releasing her. She had one shot at the timing.

A flying somersault toward the threat caused Brandy Lee to land on the spider's back. Her hand wrapped under its jaw, as she reared back with all her might. The skin and tendons tore as wails of pain screeching through the forest. She rode him like a prized bull. The head came off the shoulders, and its body collapsed to the ground. Brandy Lee rode down to a landing. She released her grip, and the head rolled off into the dirt. Brandy Lee lifted her head toward the low-lying moon.

Raven stood there in awe. Her mouth hung open in disbelief. She watched as Brandy Lee climbed off the of the insect. Raven's heart was pounding. This woman was amazing. Brandy Lee stepped closer. There was silence. Raven pulled her in for a kiss. Lips touched gingerly at first, and then the arousal became a need. Raven felt ecstatic that she was being kissed back and not slapped. They separated as fast as they had converged.

"I am-" Raven's words cut off.

"Don't you dare say you are sorry." Brandy Lee said.

The word sorry was about to slip from Raven's mouth. "No. That kiss was nice. I was about to say I am . . ." She paused, trying to figure out her feelings. "I am feeling drained. The sun is too high in the sky. I need to find shelter."

Brandy Lee blushed. "I enjoyed the kiss too." She changed the subject. "I can smell the water. We are close. Let's go set camp and hope that's the end of any spiders." Brandy Lee removed the rest of the spider web. She grabbed Raven's hand, leading them towards the lake. It wasn't typical for her to take the lead in any situation, but the sisters' blood in her heart filled her with courage.

9
Lake

With a late arrival at the lake, the sun rose high in the sky. The tree lines around the water produced very little coverage. Raven hid under a special blanket that shielded her from the sun while Brandy Lee put the tent up. She placed it on the edge of the woods, allowing the sunrays to filter between branches. Drops of rain slowed the process, and Raven's safety had her on edge to finish. Noises emerged from the depths of the woods, distracting her. She identified every animal's sound, while eyes scanned the area. Mixing with the animals were unusual sounds. She swore she heard giggling at one point. Her keen vision produced nothing, and that scared her. It was a little after seven before they crawled into the tent. Raven could barely hold her head up, and her eyes fought to stay open. Brandy

Lee helped pull her boots off, then her pants. She tucked her in the sleeping bag and watched as her eyelids grew heavy, succumbing to sleep.

An hour ago, she kissed those lips. A surge swept through her body as Brandy Lee thought of being pulled into her. Those arms around her. Breaths shared. *Stop! You can't be thinking about this woman. You have enough to think about, like not getting killed.* Brandy Lee rolled over and searched for sleep.

Raven's eyes fluttered open. She closed them again. The events from the day before ran through her mind. They made it to the lake with little resistance. Other than the birds, a black panther, and spiders, the day was an easy go.

Raven opened her eyes back up to find Brandy Lee looking at her with those toxic gold eyes. "Evening!" Raven whispered.

"Hi!" Brandy Lee whispered back. "Traveling exhausted both of us." Brandy Lee rolled over and stretched. Her tank top slipped up, revealing a toned belly. Mixed in between the solid muscles laid a three-inch scar near her rib cage. Old, ragged, and out of place on the perfect body. Raven ran a finger across it. She felt Brandy Lee shiver under the touch.

"Are you cold?" Raven asked.

"No, I am okay." Brandy Lee replied.

"How did you get this scar?"

"I don't know. I got it while I was human. But I don't remember."

Brandy Lee rolled to her side to face Raven. The covers came down, exposing her bright purple underwear. She pulled the covers up because a chill filled the air, and she was uncomfortable flashing her panties. The liquid courage was long gone. "How do you feel? The sun drained the energy from you. You had me worried." Brandy Lee's words only complimented the look in her eyes.

"I feel fine. Thanks for taking care of me and getting me inside the tent." Raven ran a finger down her arm, and Brandy Lee shivered again. "Want to talk about the kiss?" Raven couldn't help from staring at the full lips. She wanted another but needed to know if the last one was merely adrenaline.

Brandy Lee gave a shoulder shrug. Her eyes diverted to the corner of the tent. "Raven . . ." her words trailed off.

"Oh, I get it. It was just a moment thing. It's okay." Raven's words cracked a little. She had feelings for this girl. Scolding herself, how could this happen? Over the years, Raven had her share of one-night stands. Plenty of them. She was always on the lookout for that next bedpost notch. Many women filled her bed, but still it remained empty. She never developed emotions towards anyone. Since the first glance, Brandy Lee had her trying to catch a breath. Her eyes couldn't get enough of her, and her mind couldn't process being away from her. A simple touch and Raven's legs molded into jelly. *Let it go! She is not into you.* Raven scolded.

"Raven," Brandy Lee repeated with a softness. She blew out a puff of air. "I don't know what I'm doing." She whispered.

"Brandy Lee, like I said. It's okay. Let's finish the mission." Raven sat up and unlocked the bottom flap of the door. A touch of the upper arm brought her attention back. She lowered down. Their eyes met in a moment of silence.

Brandy Lee whispered, "No, I mean that I have never kissed before. That was my first kiss. I don't know how to process any of these feelings. God! This is so embarrassing."

"Your first kiss?"

Brandy Lee nodded in response.

"Did you like it?" Raven asked. She cupped her face. Her thumb stroked the soft skin of her cheek. A tear wet her finger.

Again, a head nod followed the question.

"Look at me." A lift of the chin followed. Gold and Emerald converged. "I liked it too. Can I kiss you again?" Raven didn't need words, and she didn't need a head nod. The woman's eyes lying next to her answered with desire. She leaned in, and their lips touched — a gentle kiss, with lips lingering for the time of a taken breath. Raven pulled away.

Brandy Lee laid still with her eyes closed and her heart racing. The sensation of their lips touching remained well after the kiss ended. A burst of tingles ricocheted inside her body. Heavy lids fluttered open. A teenage girl's bashful smile masked the woman's face. Their foreheads laid onto each other.

Raven laid back, pulling Brandy Lee down into her arms. "One more hour of napping before we head out. The sun will be deep into the horizon." Her fingers combed through the blonde hair. Raven whispered, "We will go slow." They fell back to sleep.

The two would have thought they were dreaming if it wasn't for the breeze that swirled inside the tent from the open door. Raven's eyes popped open wide, realizing she left the lock undone on the flap. The lock secured the tent, turning it into a tomb for her while keeping things out and burying her within. The voice went off like an alarm clock. Their bodies bolted straight into a sitting position.

At the end of their feet, the flap of the tent opened. Sticking out from it was the head of a child. Her light brown hair was long and knotted. Spots of dirt speckled her face like freckles. Between parted lips, yellow teeth glowed. Her head tilted to the left and then to the right. Her eyes scanned the tent before resting on the two women. "Come out and play?" Dingy teeth revealed a sweet smile filled with an alternative motive. She ducked out.

Raven and Brandy Lee sat there, staring at the flapping tent door. It was empty. A child? Why would a child be in this evil-filled forest?

"Um… what? Who was that?" Brandy Lee asked.

"A child?" Raven said as a question more than an answer.

It started as a distance rumble that formed into humming. It grew stronger until the noise developed words and then sentences. Finally, a song rung out. The women listened. Their heads turned to each other with widening eyes. Mouths opened. The children were singing. "Children?" They both questioned.

". . . and we all fall down."

10
Play Time

She leaned in a high arch, the cargo shorts slipping over her behind. Brandy Lee mumbled when the end of the zipper was impossible to find. Exhaling a huff of determination, she gave a yank, and the shorts zipped up. Shuffling up to her knees, she peeked outside of the tent. *There are so many. Look at all the beautiful children.*

Raven rustled behind her, trying to get on her pants in the confined space. Reprimanding herself for leaving the tent unlocked, how could she be so stupid? So careless. She had placed them in danger. The attraction to Brandy Lee was a distraction needing shelving until they made it through the forest and faced the council. She would not let her guard down again. Raven came up behind Brandy Lee in the same kneeling position. Trying to see out of the same tiny hole, she only got a face full of blonde hair. “Brandy Lee, let me see.” Raven made the request. She watched as Brandy Lee fell back on her heels. Scooting closer, Raven balanced her core with an arm around Brandy Lee’s waist, drawing an eyebrow raise from the blonde. Raven shrugged off the gesture and let her eyes scan outwards.

There were close to twenty-five children running and playing around the grounds near the tent. Little boys and girls giggled, teased, and sang in small clusters. By the lake, two boys and two girls circled, blonde hair bouncing off their shoulders. Their facial features were identical. Raven guessed they were sisters and brothers. Their little arms swung back and forth, as low voices sang out a song. A small brown-haired boy with round glasses leaned back on a log. His eyes scanned left to right without head movement, while reading a book held close to him.

Raven eyed a little girl with hair so red; the unruly strands looked like flames shooting from her head. Her face was covered in freckles; her skin the color of paste. She chased younger children around relentlessly. Using both hands, she gave a bully push to the back of the younger child who she ran down like a bull. Her targets tumbled head-over-heels, little red jumping over them in search of the next child. A wicked laugh rang out as she chose her victims. Twins kicked a ball between themselves in a corner. With hair combed to perfection and dressed in suits, their eyes squinted with each kick.

With curiosity eating at her, Brandy Lee needed to see what was going on outside. She pulled at the tent's zipper, enlarging the hole as she peeked out with Raven. Appearing was the same dirty, matted hair girl's face. They were nose-to-nose. "So, you gonna come out and play?" She said, followed by a tilt of the head. "Dontcha like us?" she asked. Her head whipped backward, and the hole was empty again.

"Okay, that's screwed up. Come on. These kids need to go on their way." Raven said. A temper sneaked out in her tone. "Or maybe we need to get moving. Either way, little children won't scare me."

"Raven, don't! They are just kids." Brandy Lee pleaded. The low hissing sound emerging from Raven alarmed her. She was afraid of what Raven might do. Such small humans could not be a threat. They just wanted to play.

Stepping from the tent, Raven felt her foot catch the bottom where the material stuck up. Falling forward with flailing arms, she fell face forward into the dirt. Raven closed her eyes. She released the longest puff of air with her cheeks expanding to their limits. *Damn it!* She thought. She pushed up on both hands.

"Are you okay?" Brandy Lee asked, joining her

outside. The moon was full and glistened off the lake. She raised her face towards the round ball in the sky.

"Fine," Raven answered with gritted teeth. She was already up and brushing the dirt from her pants. Her hands stopped in a mid-brush when silence fell. A lift of her eyes revealed all the children standing and staring at her. They stood still. The balls had stopped bouncing. No giggling; no running; singing ceased. Over the silence, the background sound of flopping fish in the lake echoed. Raven stood up straight. Her eyes studied each face intensely. Reaching out, she pulled Brandy Lee closer to her.

The little boy tugged at her pants leg, which caused Raven to pull back. "Hi," He said. It was the little boy from the log. He looked up at the two women through his round glasses. He clung to the book that rested under his armpit. "My name is Theo. What's yours?" His eyes traveled from Brandy Lee and Raven and then back. Raven noticed his head still didn't move. Only the solid whites of his eyes shifted side to side.

"Something wrong with your neck?" Raven blurted the question out before she could pull the words back in. The warning came with a punch in her arm, rendered by Brandy Lee of her bluntness. A roll of her eyes, and Raven closed her lips into a tight line.

Brandy Lee lowered down to one knee, meeting

Theo eye to eye. Raven cringed at the closeness but kept her eyes on the other children that had gone back to playing. She wanted to pack the tent up and get the hell out of there. Overall, the kids didn't seem like a threat, but they were in a magical forest where nothing is what it seems. Reaching the She-Wolf Council was the priority, instead of playing with kids. With a lot of miles yet to go, Raven was ready to get started. Unfortunately, Brandy Lee was on a different agenda.

"Hi, Theo; my name is Brandy Lee. This lady is Raven. Where'd you come from? Why are you here?"

Theo shrugged his shoulders. "We're the lost children of the Never-Evers."

"Never-Evers? I don't understand." Brandy Lee asked.

Theo shrugged his little shoulder again, his eyes fixated on the ground. "I don't know. We live here by the lake. It is our home." He lifted his arm, pointing his stubby finger towards the dark woods that stood beyond the lake. "We don't go there. It's scary."

The sudden bump caused Raven to wobble sideways. She looked down at the bright redheaded little girl that was trying relentlessly to tip her over. Raven lifted an eyebrow at the small nuisance. The little girl stuck her tongue out, pushing again before running off. Raven took a step towards a chase but got stopped by an elbow grab. She turned to find Brandy Lee shaking her head side to side. Once again, Raven could only release a sigh of frustration.

"That's Red. Sorry; she can be a bully." Theo's voice broke the eye contact between the two women. Their eyes drifted back towards him. They watched him search the surrounding by moving his entire body in a clockwise motion. The blondes over there are the Smittens. They are siblings. Those are the twins, Andy and Randy. He continued turning on his heel, introducing the other kids; so many names that would not get remembered.

"Hi! Wanna play?" The familiar voice asked. It was the little girl that stuck her head in their tent. She wore a dirty blue dress, ragged from years worn. Her black shoes scuffed from playing and hair in disarray.

When Theo took a step sideways, the girl stepped in front of Brandy Lee. "This is Pigpen Peggy." He announced.

"Ready to play?" Peggy asked. She batted her ocean blue eyes.

"What do you want to play?" Brandy Lee asked.

"Pin the tail on the donkey." Peggy answered.

"We don't have that game, Pigpen Peggy." Theo chimed in. The little girl pouted. Brandy Lee wondered if it was because of the name-calling.

"She can be the donkey," Peggy said while

pointing at Raven. "We can pin sticks in her hiney." Peggy giggled.

"You are not sticking anything in me. Brandy Lee, let's go. We are wasting the moonlight." The harshness in her voice was loud and clear. She was at her limit. Raven turned on her heels, heading back to the tent to pack. She would not spend one more minute playing games. She tried to figure out what was going on in Brandy Lee's mind. There was a mission, one that may change the world, but that seemed to be the last thing on her mind. Why she remained so engrossed over these kids was a mystery.

Brandy Lee ignored the stomping off by Raven and lowered her body to a log. Theo sat beside her and Peggy in front of her. "How about a quick game of rock, paper, scissors?" She asked.

"I don't know that game," Peggy answered as she crossed her legs and scooted closer. The excitement filled her voice.

She took her time explaining the game to Theo and Peggy. Before long, the Smittens, the twins, an even Red were sitting in a semi-circle listening. Their little hands were mimicking the shapes. Before long, the siblings played together, and the twins were attempting the game. Theo and Red challenged each other, while Brandy Lee and Peggy played. Raven watched at a distance as she took the tent down. Silence blanketed the night, except for the chanting of four words.

Rocks. Papers. Scissors. Shoot!

11

Let's Eat

Pulling the bandana from her back pocket, Raven wiped the sweat off the back of her neck. The night was sweltering. She tossed back a bottle of blood for nourishment. Looking over the top of the container, she observed Brandy Lee playing peek-a-boo with Pigpen Peggy. She released an inner giggle at the name. Raven's eyes searched. It was the first time she inspected the area. The water was crystal blue with the moonlight gleaming off the still surface. Raven lifted her eyes to the woods, and a shiver rolled over her spine. Her body went around in a circular motion with her eyes piercing pass the shadows. Someone was watching them. She could feel them.

A noise to her left caused her to jump. "Fuck! You scared me."

“Fuck. You scared me.” The words repeated, coming with a tilt of the head.

“Don’t say naughty words. It’s not nice. Bad boy.” Raven sounded more like she was correcting a puppy rather than talking to a little boy.

“You said it first. Bad girl.” His brother responded.

“I know that.” Raven looked at the two boys. “But that doesn’t...” Raven stopped her words, shaking her head before bringing it to a hanging still. Her eyes closed, and she inhaled as deep as her lungs would allow. A discussion composed of nonsense with a child would not happen. She pulled out her ponytail and retied it. The tying of the hair wasn’t necessary, but it brought her attention somewhere else.

“I’s Randy; this is Andy.” One twin said.

A quick look over and Raven realized the boys were identical to the last freckle, their brown hair combed to the side. Not a hair out of place. Perfect. In their brown highwater pants and yellow suspenders, it was impossible to tell them apart. Although, Raven didn’t want to try much. With one swoop, she tossed the backpack over her shoulder. She took a step to the side only to have Andy jump in front of her. His three-foot body blocked her exit.

“Can you teach us how to tie shoes?” Andy’s eyes fell to his feet. The black shoelace unraveled and hung on the ground.

"What?" Raven asked.

"Tie. Help us learn." He wiggled his foot in the air, the string dangling.

Raven huffed. *Really?* She thought. "You are serious?" In rhythm, both young boys shook their head in a yes motion. With another puff of air, Raven tossed the bag to the ground. She sat cross-legged, and in a few seconds, both boys joined her. A quick look around, and her eyes fell on Brandy Lee, who was watching. Raven received a smile of approval from the blonde hair beauty. *Maybe I will earn points for this.*

"Okay, it is a few steps." Raven started the lesson. "Crisscross pull. Loop and circle. Through the hole and loop again. Then pull."

Both boys listened as Raven repeated the procedure over and over. Little fingers mimicked with failed attempts followed by another. Frustration and determination blanketed their freckled faces. Their eyes squinted to tiny slits. Then it happened. With a pull, they both tied their shoes.

"We did it! We did it!" They screamed.

Raven couldn't help but smile. She felt a hand touch her shoulder, and Brandy Lee stood above her. Raven looked up with a cocky smile. She must have earned those brownie points because she received a soft kiss on the cheek as a reward. The lingering kiss sent a quiver to her center. She wanted so much to turn her head, take those lips onto hers and claim her, while letting their tongues swirl.

"So, that's okay?" Brandy Lee's voice shattered Raven's thoughts.

"Is what okay?" The tone in her voice displayed aggravation. The story in her thoughts was getting exciting before being interrupted.

"They want us to eat with them."

"No. What? No!" Raven shook her head rapidly from left to right. "We need to get going. We have food for you in the bag. You know I can go days without human food." By now, Raven was standing next to Brandy Lee. "Let's leave."

"Just this one last thing and I promise we will leave right after we eat." Brandy Lee's finger made a cross over the top of her heart. "I promise."

Raven bit at her lower lip. "Someone is watching us."

"And you are right. Look around. The dark forest surrounds us. I feel safe here. We can trust the children. They won't hurt us. Dinner? Just dinner and we leave." The pouty lip that Brandy Lee was giving was too much for Raven to handle. She stepped closer. The thought of nibbling that lip during passion sent an electric shock straight between her legs. She stepped closer. "What are you doing?" Brandy Lee asked.

"I am about to kiss you."

“Here?” She whispered.

“Yes, right here.” Raven slipped her hand up, Brandy Lee’s neck and under her hair. She leaned, allowing her mouth to take hers. This kiss differed from the one earlier — so much heat. Raven felt Brandy Lee give herself, causing Raven to moan. She didn’t mean to let it escape, but she never felt this feeling. There was no woman in her life that caused this uncontrollable desire. It didn’t matter that they were in the middle of a dark forest, or that children surrounded them. This moment was the one that mattered.

Giggling sounded all around. Snickering and whispering followed. A few of the children broke out in the kissing song. “K-I-S-S-I-N-G.”

Brandy Lee pulled away. “The kids.” She whispered in Raven’s ear.

Raven touched their two foreheads together. With heavy breaths, she pulled away. “Dinner, and then we will leave.”

Brandy Lee smiled. “Absolutely.”

The forest won’t kill me. My attraction to you will do the trick.

His belly shook before he took a step. He wobbled in his dirty apron around the long picnic table, serving up the unidentifiable soup out of a silver bowl. His stubby fingers dipped out a full serving of the brown liquid with strings of meat hanging over the side of the dipper. Raven cringed. When the little guy reached her, she held her hand out over the top of her bowl to stop the offering. Brandy Lee nudged her shoulder, and Raven removed her hand. She gazed at the chunk of meat swimming around her bowl. Her nose twitched.

"I'm not eating that shit." She said with a slight lean into Brandy Lee.

"Be nice." Brandy Lee said through gritted teeth. The Smittens siblings were sitting across from them. The four sat there with the same smile watching Raven and Brandy Lee. Brandy Lee smiled back. She admitted that they were odd. Their toe head blond hair reminded her of a horror film. The movie freaked her out so bad that she tried to convince her mother to dye her hair black. Beside her sat Theo and Red, and the twins sat beside Raven.

"Where are you headed?" Theo asked. His question blurted out was but not directed toward either woman. He continued to slurp up the soup as he waited for an answer.

Raven spoke first. They couldn't afford to divulge too much information. In a few minutes, all this would be behind them. “We need to get on the other side of the woods. We’re looking for a friend that got lost. You didn’t see him, did you? Brown hair, six feet tall, muscles, and wearing jeans and a plaid shirt.” Raven spit the bogus person from her mouth like water.

All the children shook their heads. “We didn’t see anyone. That friend - why is he here? The woods can be scary. We don’t go in them.”

“We don’t know.” Raven said.

Brandy Lee could hear the frustration building in Raven. She lifted her head to the moon. They had five more hours of moonlight and maybe another hour of the low sun that Raven could tolerate. Raven’s eyes pleaded to leave. The woman had had enough. It was time to say goodbye to their friends and head out.

She started to stand, and Raven was a millisecond behind her, lifting herself from the table. The kids' faces began to pout. Two of the Smittens began to cry. One twin held onto Raven’s leg; his little arms wrapped in a vice. It was Theo that spoke.

“We have something to give you before heading out. It may help with your journey. It has helped us from some animals in the forest. Come on; follow us.” Theo’s tiny hand slipped into Brandy Lee’s hand, and with a pull, they headed off to one side of the lake. Raven didn’t have a choice but to follow.

They reached an area with overgrown vines and greenage that appeared to be a tunnel. The hole was dark, and visibility was low. Raven bent at the hips and looked deep into the dark space. "We're not going in there," She announced. With a grab of the hand, she pulled Brandy Lee in the opposite direction. Theo and Red countered with their pull.

"It's safe in there. It is just a place we keep things. Trust me. It will help you against any evil which you may face." The words were so pure and innocent that Brandy Lee couldn't help but let her hand slip from Raven. Raven grabbed it back and tightened her grip.

"Just let me look, and we will be on our way. It may help," Brandy Lee said.

With a sink of the heart, Raven let go. She watched as Brandy Lee ducked low to enter the dark tunnel. Every bone in her body told her something wasn't right. And in that instant, she received her confirmation.

The gate slammed closed with metal hitting metal. A screeching sound of the door locked in place, echoing into the air. The gate, large and rustic, seemed untouched for years. A scream from Brandy Lee seared through Raven's body. She stepped forward. She heard a click just as the pain knocked the wind from her. A bright light illuminated her vision. The light brightened the night like the sun, causing Raven's legs to crumble as pain seared through her body. The sun? The glow shone so bright that she doubled on the ground in a fetal position. Her hand reached for the unseen Brandy Lee before the world went dark.

12
Captured

"Raven! Raven! Open your eyes." Her eyes moved frantically, searching the cage that held her imprisoned. Tall enough to stand upright and long enough to pace. She pulled at the rusty old bars, but it would not budge. *I have fucked up now. What the hell have I gotten us into?* Raven stood fifty feet from her. Her arms were bound with her body wrapped in a greenage that held her to a stake. A floodlight shined on her. Her head was drooping, and long strands of brown hair covered her face. Brandy Lee paced back and forth like a caged animal. She needed to figure out how in the hell to get out of here while controlling the inner wolf that wanted to appear.

The round glasses appeared from the dark with a glow, followed by the bright red hair. One by one, the children arrived. They stared at them like a hunter stares at their kill. Theo shifted his eyes from one woman to the next. “Wake her!” He ordered one twin. All eyes watched as the rays from the bulb dimmed.

Raven stirred.

“Hey-” The brown hair freckled twin said before he poked her in the stomach.

“Hey-” The other twin picked up a stick and stabbed her leg.

“Stop that!” Brandy Lee screamed. “I swear…”

“You swear what?” Red ran her finger over the bars at the other end of the cage. Brandy Lee jumped towards her, but Red was too fast and moved away. She wiggled her index finger from side to side. “Uh, uh,” Red twisted her head, following the trail of Brandy Lee’s eyes. Their eyes fixated on the dirty little girl. Peggy found it hard to hold their look. Red laughed out loud, breaking the trance between the blonde and matted-hair child. “You think she will help you. That’s the funniest thing I have heard all day. That little mouse wouldn’t help you if you were the last person on earth.” Red spun on her heel and joined Theo.

Raven stirred again.

“Raven, wake the hell up.” Brandy Lee hollered.

Andy walked and stood under Raven. He bent at the waist and stared up at Raven’s face. Her hair hid her features. With the sunlight machine on low, a shadow cast on the side of her face. Andy poked at her stomach again. This time her eyes widened, her head lifted, and she snapped at Andy's head. Her fangs missed his face by a hair's breadth. The second snap missed by a mile as he flailed his arms and tumbled backward.

Laughter erupted.

Raven's emerald eyes glowed as she scanned the area. Her strength cut in half, and mistletoe tied her to the stake. The greenage that delivered many kisses at Christmas was a vampire's weakness. Her eyes held anger while moving her head from one child to another. A few turned away; some grinned. Some stared back with the same fed rage. It was within seconds that her thoughts went to Brandy Lee. Where was she? Lucky, with a twist of the head, their eyes met.

The sorrow and shame in Brandy Lee's eyes were as bright as the low moon. She mouthed, "I am sorry." Their predicament was her fault. They should have left long ago. She wished she had listened to Raven. It was her soft side that put them in danger. Her love for kids was the culprit. Growing up in foster care, she played big sister to the younger children in the home. She wanted children of her own, but that dream vanished. Like so many, once it was revealed she was a she-wolf, the dream disappeared. Only human women could have children, and because all males were human, that eliminated any chance of a vampire or a wolf reproducing.

"Are you okay?" Raven asked.

"Yes, but the cage is silver. I can't break it." Brandy Lee responded.

Raven turned her attention to the ringleader. Her eyes glared at Theo. "What do you want?" Raven hissed out. A burst of light blinded her, just as the pain seared through her body. Her head fell back in agony. Andy recovered from his fall and sat at the flood lamp, the knob on full blast. A grin stretched across his face — revenge for the embarrassment that he suffered.

The suffering watched from a distance filled Brandy Lee helplessness. Wetness flowed down her cheek, and she wiped at her face. Her heart was about to explode from the pain.

"Andy, stop!" Theo snapped the order. He watched as the light dimmed again.

Raven hissed. "I will kill you." Her breath heavy.

"Why are you doing this?" Brandy Lee yelled.

Everyone's attention jerked. Theo circled with his hands behind his back. His eyes stared at the ground. "Why? Why? Why? They always ask the same question. It is simple. You're our sacrifice. See, if we give the Lake Witch a sacrifice, then we get to live here. Fear free. Oh, and trust me, a she-wolf and a vampire would get us paid-up for years."

"You little shit. When I get free, I'll rip your..."

Red cut her words off. "I don't think you are in a position to make threats. If you don't calm down, then Andy and Randy will be glad to turn up the lights." She raised her eyebrows.

Theo stepped in front of Andy, their eyes inches apart. The glare deep. Andy folded. He stepped back, and with a bite of the lower lip, he took his place beside his brother. Theo turned on both heels, clapping his hands together. "Okay, that's enough playing. Listen up, you two. The Lake Witch will be here tomorrow. Sooo . . . Let's all get along. We will not hurt you. You are no good to us as damaged goods. So, Raven, we will cover you soon with that special blanket that you are carrying around for protection from the sun. Behave, and tomorrow it will be all over." Theo started to walk away before Raven's words stopped him.

"You're not a child, are you? None of you are." Raven asked.

Theo stopped with his back to her. Moments clicked by before he spoke. "No, we are not." He spun around. "Frozen in the age of when we arrived at the lake. We remained seized in a child's body, so that we won't run away. None of us would last a day in the Dark Forest in these pathetic bodies. Does that answer your question?"

"Well, it makes me feel better. This way, when I slit your throat, I won't feel too bad."

Theo released a belly laugh. The other children giggled and snorted along. He couldn't count how many times the sacrifice threatened him. Grant you, most of the previous victims were drunken college students that entered the forest on a dare. Urban legends of the evil that lurked in The Dark Forest proceeded itself. Laughter slowed, and Theo's thoughts went back to the day his life became part of that camp-fire scary story. The group of them were traveling when a tornado dropped from the clouds, and in a split second, they were tossing and turning. With the wind the strength of ten lions, they swirled like rag dolls. They fell into the lake. Some members of the group perished, including Theo's and Red's wife. The two wives were sisters, thus, bonding Theo and Red for life.

Ridden with grief was the door of opportunity. The Lake Witch needed to place a spell on them without a fight. The lake became the jail, and thereby the bodies became their restraints. They got summoned to feed the witch with any dupe captured. This ritual kept them safe and away from landing on the witch's dinner table as the main course.

With a heavy sigh and the slightest hint of empathy, he raised his eyes and shifted them around, not moving his neck. The neck injury was courtesy of the free fall from the twister that dropped him from the sky. With his lips making a thin line, and eyes that went black as coal, he ordered, "Cover her up. The sun is close. Tomorrow evening we present our gift to the Lake Witch with the hopes of freedom." Theo turned, walking away. Red followed suit. Their silhouettes melted into the shadows.

The Smittens each grabbed an end of the blanket. Spreading it out, they formed a large rectangle. With a quick lift of the arms, the coverage rose like a parachute. The material fell over Raven, covering her head to toe. The four of them grabbed mistletoe, skipping and dancing around her while tying the blanket to her.

Just like that, silence echoed.

"Raven!" Brandy Lee whispered. "Can you hear me?"

"I can."

"Are you okay? The sun is up." Brandy Lee said, lifting her face to the fireball in the sky.

"I am fine. The cover is protecting me. Are you okay?"

"Yes, just wanting to rip these bars apart. What are we going to do?"

"There is nothing we can do until tomorrow. Not with the sun high." Raven answered in frustration.

"I should've listened to you." Brandy Lee's voice quivered.

"Don't cry. Please don't. I will figure a way out of this. I need to think about it. You have my promise. We'll not die here." Raven did not know what the plan was, but she would think of something. No make-believe child or witch would be the end of her. Nor the end of a relationship with Brandy Lee that she was planning to explore.

"Raven," Brandy Lee whispered.

"Yes-" Raven said back.

"I like you. Like, I mean, I like you." Brandy Lee said. Once again, a quiver rattled in her words, but this rattle was from nerves.

Raven smiled a hidden smile. Her wording sounded like a middle-school-age girl. She knew it took some mustering for her to say those words. "I like you too. There is something about you that makes me feel alive. Your lips, eyes, and kiss had me from the start. When we get out of this - I mean the whole forest - I want to spend time with you and get to know you. You are one of the sexiest creatures that I have ever seen. You make me feel whole." Silence filled the air. "Brandy Lee, is something wrong. Did I say something to upset you?"

"No. I am blushing."

"That must be a sight. I wish I could see the redness."

"You will — one day. I can tell you are getting tired. Sleep. When the moon rises, we will fight."

13

Lake Witch

Complete darkness smothers . . .

The ties that bound her released and, with a quick yank, the cover that protected her flipped off. The moon was bright. Raven opened her eyes to find all the children in a semi-circle. An arrangement of rocks and twigs laid on a table about fifty feet away. *An odd mixture for the ceremony,* Raven thought. She remained tied to the stake. Her legs and arms felt like wet noodles. Half her strength was drained from the sunlight lamp which shone against her body.

"Good morning, ladies." Theo grabbed their attention.

Brandy Lee was slow to rise. She stretched, trying to relieve the pain from stiffening bones. The metal floor in the cage was hard and made the day long. Her blonde hair tousled like a one-night stand. Brandy Lee stood.

"We've about an hour before the Lake Witch arrives. So, let's get you ladies cleaned up." Theo motioned the women to get busy.

Red, the two female Smittens, and Pigpen Peggy made their way to the table. Pigpen Peggy arranged the twigs in a bowl, four diagonals and four verticals. Her fingers repeated the design in the second bowl. The Smittens leaned over the table, twisting the rocks over the twigs. The loud, crunching noise echoed over the lake. A red flame burst from a long match as Red stroked it across the table. A flick of the hand and the glow of the fire filled the bowls. Black smoke billowed upwards, filling the air. The smoke twisted and swirled into shapes. The other children's voices rang out in awe. The four girls split into pairs, and with a turn of the heels, they headed towards Raven and Brandy Lee.

Chanting began. "Auda, Mone, Tila, Shaname." The girls circled their captives, repeating the chant over and over. Black smoke circled the two captured bodies. The smell was unbearable to the nostrils, causing both women to gag at the odor. After four slow circles, their steps reversed the path, and the chant flipped. "Shaname, Tila, Mone, Auda." the girls chanted.

Brandy Lee's eyes pursued Peggy as she followed Red in a circle. The pain and hurt transferring from Peggy to Brandy Lee. Brandy Lee's heart ached for the young girl. Peggy was just as much a victim as she and Raven. The women finished and walked to stand behind Theo. His smug smile gleamed in the moonlight.

"We'll be back in thirty minutes, and the party will begin. Let's eat." One by one, the children followed him away, all except Peggy.

Peggy stood at a distance staring at Brandy Lee. Her big eyes filled with fear. She pushed her matted hair away from her face before wiping at her eyes with her sleeve.

"Peggy, it's okay. Come here." The words whispered loudly.

Raven murmured under her breath. "Grab her when she gets close."

"No, I won't." Brandy Lee responded.

"Fuck. I'm scared. Grab her ass." Raven mumbled back.

Peggy kicked at the ground. Her eyes looked at the worn shoes, and her fingers played with the dirty torn dress. "I'm sorry." The words barely muttered out.

"Let us go. We can get you out of here. I promise. We will take you away with us. There is a better world beyond this lake." Brandy Lee tossed the promises out. Time was running out.

"Theo will kill me. Red will torture me. I know of the other world. I don't belong there anymore."

Peggy kicked more dirt around. She felt her heart skip a few beats. She wanted to help her new friends, but the fear ravishing her body was crippling.

"Peggy, unlock the fucking gate," Raven yelled.

Peggy backed up. She froze. Suddenly, she shifted in a surprise move. Peggy stepped in front of the lock of Brandy Lee's cage. Her hands fiddled with the combination. She rotated the first number and the lock click. With a twist, the second number fell in place. One more. One more was all it would take to free Brandy Lee. Peggy's turned her head in search of a watcher. Raven and Brandy Lee's heart pounded with each motion of the lock. The air was thick, and breaths came hard. Hope was rising.

The red blur sprung from the dark shadows, catching Peggy in the mid-section. Her body hit the ground hard, as a puff of dirt encircled her and Red. They tumbled with legs intertwined. The air knocked from her lungs; Peggy gasped. Fingers around her throat tightened, and she was looking into the eyes of rage. Red hovered over her. The fingers tightened, and the air became scarce. She couldn't speak. Her arms scraped at the outstretched arms of her attacker. Her grasp became weaker and weaker as the world around her went black.

"Red! Let her go!" Theo screamed as he ran across the yard in a huff. Sliding to a stop beside her, the dirt puffing in a cloud again. He grabbed at her arm, but Red was not letting go. Her mindset remained on one thing. Kill Pigpen Peggy. Theo's eyes searched around for something, anything, to make her release the vice hold. He didn't care about Pigpen Peggy; he wanted her for a sacrifice. Reaching down by his feet, he picked up the boulder, swinging his arm in a circle. The rock came down, cracking Red's skull. She slumped over. *Shit, that was too hard,* he cursed himself.

Peggy coughed and gasped. Grunting, she pushed the dead body off her. Her body curled into a fetal position with her eyes closed. Cold air surrounded her body. The temperature dropped twenty degrees. Goosebumps trickled over her arms, as hair lifted on the back of her neck. Her eyes widened into huge circles, and she pushed up on her arms, with her eyes skimming the water. She was here. The Lake Witch was a breath away.

Raven and Brandy Lee watched the lake as the transformation began. Ripples turned into waves; blue water turned black as soot. Multiple times the liquid rose into the air, swirling into a sculpture. Each piece of art took the form of a human. Just as the girls started to recognize facial features; the water dumped back into the blackened pool.

At the shore's edge, the water pulled back. She arrived. A tiny black dress hugged her body, with marine foliage dangling from her arms. Her eyes black as the water that birthed her. Hair, the color of the night, moved with a life of its own. At first glance, it appeared the wind blew the wet strands. With every step onshore, those moving strands became water snakes. With bodies intertwining, they hissed and snapped at each other with eyes that matched their master.

"What the fuck?" Raven said out loud. She started to yank harder on the vines that held her wrist, searching for an escape. When she looked back up, the Lake Witch was inches from her face. Her breath smelled of stagnant water. She studied Raven.

"A vampire." She hissed like the snakes on her head. "What a treat."

"And a she-wolf," Theo added from a distance.

The Lake Witch floated over to the bars that held Brandy Lee. Her long fingers wrapped around the steel, as she placed her face between two bars. Her tongue slithered from between her lips, flicking into the air. "You're not in your natural form."

A pluck of her hair and a snake wiggled into the cage. It slithered around in circles before standing straight up. Releasing a hiss, it jumped towards Brandy Lee. She backed into the corner. The snake lunged, and she hurdled to the side. Her anger tipped the scale. Jumping into the air, Brandy Lee came down on all fours. Standing in the cage was a majestic white wolf. Long smooth fur covered her body. Her well-defined muscles revealed the power behind them.

Her teeth, as white as snow, glistened with salvia. She growled, and saliva hit the ground as it dripped from her canines. Her large paws took a step towards the snake. One swift move and the snake became pinned under the massive foot. It wiggled wildly under crippling pressure. Almost human screams emerged from the seized reptile. The wolf's eyes fell to its prey and snapped. The snake divided into two pieces with the head between Brandy Lee's jaws. She tossed the head to the side. In the same motion, she leaped at the witch, snapping her powerful jaws.

Pulling away, she laughed. "Oh, impressive. You'll be a fine addition to my collection of souls." As the words slipped from her lips, she stroked her hair. The snakes wrapped around her fingers. They were the people she killed in the past. That was why the snake's screams sounded human.

Brandy Lee circled the cage. She stopped to look over at Raven. Her golden eyes, the only resemblance of her, stared deep into Raven's emerald eyes. *What do we do?* Brandy Lee thought.

Raven's eyes widened when she heard the thought develop in Brandy Lee's head. She could hear her thoughts. Raven smiled and answered. "I don't know. But this bitch of a witch will die."

You can hear me? Silent words asked.

Yes. That must be the gift that Queen Lana gave

me before I left. I can hear your thoughts and talk to you.

I better be careful of what I think of then. Keep my thoughts clean.

Raven laughed out loud. A witch with snakes for hair was about to eat them, and Brandy Lee cracked a joke. Perfect. Another reason to fall in love with this woman.

Lake Witch squinted her eyes in disbelief. Of all her years of terror, no one ever laughed. “Laugh now because it is all about to change. Prepare your sacrifice for me!” The Lake Witch screamed the order. The children started to move in different directions. Except for Red, who remained in a puddle of blood on the ground.

14
Run

Darken clouds rolled across the sky. The Lake Witch stood in front of Raven, arms outstretched. She summoned her army. They responded like perfect soldiers. Hundreds of black water snakes squirmed their way from the water. They all stayed behind the witch, waiting for the command to feed.

"It's time for you to be a part of me. I'll assume your powers. You'll live with me as one of my servants." The Lake Witch lifted her arms. Thunder rolled.

A flash of light sent electricity blazing through the ground with smoke rising. Everyone, including the snakes, jumped at nature's fury. The black blur was unnoticed until the last minute since the power behind the voltage was so distracting. The black panther landed between the witch and Raven, releasing a deafening roar.

The cat, pushing off on her legs, landed in the witch's chest. Their bodies tumbled into the snakes, causing them to flee back into the lake. The panther's jaws clamped down onto the right arm as her head shook from left to right. The panther pulled the witch across the dirt, kicking and screaming.

All the children huddled in the corner. Their bodies shivered with fear, frozen in their tracks. Except, Pigpen Peggy. She ran in a vast circle to avoid the twisting pile of fur, arms, and legs while hurdling snakes that snapped at her. She reached the cage where the white wolf stood watching the chaos from inside. She only needed to roll the combination to the last number to unlock the gate. Her fingers trembled, and the lock shook in her hand. She twisted, and a click sounded out. Her hands wrapped around the bars and pulled, allowing the door to swing open.

Brandy Lee stepped forward. Her head turned, and her golden eyes met those of Peggy's. Then her head turned towards Raven before turning back to Peggy. Her way of telling Peggy to free her friend. Brandy Lee released a growl deep from her throat and ran towards the fight. Arriving, she wasted no time attacking. Her leg stomped down on the fighting witch, pinning her body to the ground. The evil woman's strength was no match for the wolf.

The black panther let go of her bite, hissing at Brandy Lee. For a time, it appeared the two beasts were about to clash over the prey. Brandy Lee hunched, and a slow vibrating growl escaped. The panther swatted at the air with her claws, but then coward down. She was backing up in a crouch with locked eyes on the competition. A twist of the body, the panther jumped towards the black snakes which were emerging back from the lake. Brandy Lee straddled the witch with her body hovering over. She laid bleeding from multiple bites wreathing in pain. Her magical powers reduced to a few flickers. Lowering her head with powerful jaws inches from the witch's face, drool dripped between clenched teeth onto the witch. The upper lip raised and moved as a thunderous rumble rolled out into the night from deep inside Brandy Lee. Her mouth parted, and the death was over in seconds. She stretched her neck up and a howl released into the night.

Raven arrived as the witch's life ceased. Her body's strength drained from mistletoe and the lamp; she fell to the ground under the wobbly legs. Brandy Lee ran over, rubbing her head into her cheek. *Are you okay?*

"I'm weak. Let's get the hell out of here." Raven whispered as she caressed the side of Brandy Lee's head. With everything that happened, she took notice of the softness of the fur between her fingers.

It felt like an exquisite bear rug. So soft. So sensual.

Yes, let's go. Brandy Lee gave another nudge with her head.

As they looked toward the lake, the snakes were retreating into the water. The black panther held a few squirming reptiles between clasped jaws. One bite and the heads were severed. The cat tossed the decapitated head back into the lake. The children huddled in the same corner, but an illness ravished their bodies. They held their stomachs in pain. They were growing. The spell that hovered over them for years had been erased with the Lake Witch's death. Raven and Brandy Lee watched the transformation as the children turned into grown-ups. All ages but they looked the same. The Smittens were all blonde-haired siblings, but now, two women and two men in their twenties. The twins remained identical, which made telling them apart harder than before.

Theo stepped from the shadows, rage set in his eyes. He was a handsome man in his thirties. Was he upset? He was free of the witch and the spell. Free to leave the lake. "You've taken everything from me. My woman and my power over this pathetic group." Theo turned to Red after the deaths of their spouses. They'd instilled fear into the others, controlling the small clan of children. Appeasing the witch was a mere nuisance throughout the time. It was the power they craved.

With the witch dead, spell erased, and Red dead, Theo was no longer needed. The others were not at his mercy and could stand on their own. “I will kill you!” He screamed while lifting his arms.

Brandy Lee and Raven didn’t see when the beautiful woman appeared. Her straight combed light brown hair cascaded over her shoulders. She was young, possibly twenty. Where dirt once stained her face, freckles now replaced. Her curves were hypnotizing. She was breathtaking. It was Peggy. She turned her head for a moment, but long enough to catch the attention of the two women. Her arms lifted; the air becoming chilled as a wall of ice formed. It was solid and thick, locking Theo on the other side. His figure could be seen banging on the frozen liquid with muffled threats whispering from behind the wall. Peggy turned around. “Go. This wall will not hold him for long.”

Raven stepped forward. “Peggy, you are a fairy?”

“We all are, but there is no time for this. Go.”

“Come with us!” Raven said.

“I don’t know what there is for me out there.” She answered. The cracking of the ice drew her attention away.

Enough was enough, and Brandy Lee was done with it all. Nudging her nose between the legs of Peggy, and with a swift toss, her body went flying. A gasp escaped from the young girl as she landed on the back of the white wolf. Brandy Lee felt fingers grasping at her fur, as Peggy tried to find a balance. She looked at Raven. *Get on!* She told her. Raven jumped up, spooning Peggy with arms wrapped around her. *Tell her to hold on!* Another thought sent to Raven.

"Brandy Lee says to hold on." Raven tightens her grip.

A quick scan of the area by Brandy Lee, and she noticed the lake didn't look as friendly or inviting as when they first arrived. She walked over to the book bag that laid a few feet away. Taking the strap by her mouth, she tossed it behind her to Raven. Her eyes scanned their escape. Crawling into the woods was the black panther. She wanted nothing to do with her, so she leaped to the right and headed in the opposite direction. The ice wall crashed to the ground as she reached the tree line. Without a glance backward, the three disappeared into the shadows of the Dark Forest, leaving the lake behind them.

15

Hello

Paws pounded into the ground with every step; the pace fast and dangerous. It wasn't until a tug on the fur that made Brandy Lee slow down. There couldn't be enough distance between them and the lake. She slowed and stopped in a clearing. With panting breaths, she lowered to her belly and the two passengers jumped off. She laid her head on her front legs when a tender touch stroked her neck. Her eyes closed for a minute while the realization surfaced. She had taken a life, and the residue of blood simmered her mouth. She whimpered. Then, as if Raven felt her pain, a whisper filled in her ear.

"You did what you had to do. Relax and come back to me in your human form. I'm stronger now and can protect us. Changing has you tired and weak. I got you, Baby. Now, let me see that beautiful face."

With her words, Brandy Lee shifted into her human state. Her naked body collapsed. Catching her mid-fall, Raven embraced her. She held and rocked the exhausted woman in her arms, whispering reassuring words as Brandy Lee cried uncontrollably. The flood of emotions so intense, the woman shook. Peggy squatted down beside the two.

"I'll make you a shower. Would you like that Brandy Lee?" A head nod confirmed. Peggy stood and raised her arms above her head. In a circular motion that grew with speed, water appeared. It swirled above in turmoil in a small tornado of liquid. A jerk of her arms in a downward motion and the water cascaded towards the ground. A controlled stream of water developed into a shower.

Raven watched the magic in awe. She read about fairies in school, but it was rare to see one. Never mind the fact she was watching one's magic. The magic of this creature was the most powerful in the world. The thought of the Lake Witch imprisoning one was astonishing, but a whole frollick was unbelievable. Raven gave Peggy a soft smile. Then, she lifted Brandy Lee in one scoop. She walked into the water and placed Brandy Lee's feet on the ground. The warm water cascaded over them like summer rain. The day washed away. Usually, being this close to a beautiful naked woman would have Raven ripping off her own clothes, but today, she wanted only to make sure Brandy Lee remained safe.

After the shower, Raven dressed Brandy Lee and helped her into the tent which Peggy had set up. She leaned on one elbow, watching her eyelids get heavy. She stroked the sleepy woman's cheek. "You look so tired," Raven said in a soft voice. A hand raised touching her upper arm.

"Heck of a day. I had to fix what I screwed up." Brandy Lee said.

"Don't be silly. We both fell for the charades. It is past us now. We get our strength back and will continue towards the council. Get the answers we need and cancel the kill order on you. You need to rest." Raven's emerald eyes looked loving down at the weaken girl. She was falling hard for her. The next move caught her off guard, taking Raven's breath away. Brandy Lee wrapped her fingers around the back of Raven's neck and pulled her into a kiss. A soft touch of the lips raged into their mouths, parting ever so allowing tongues to twirl. Taking all her strength, Raven pulled away from the most delicious kiss that ever touched her lips. A peck on the cheek and Raven whispered, "Now rest." With those two words, she watched as Brandy Lee's eyelids grew heavy and drooped. Sleep took control.

Her eyes searched for the moon as she stepped from the tent. There was close to two-and-a-half hours left before the sun would rise. The clearing provided very little protection from the ball of heat. Raven's blanket had been left behind at the lake, and with the tent her only barrier, she would have to be careful. Moving forward would require careful planning on their parts. The last obstacle they need was for her crisping like bacon in a frying pan. Raven stretched and then made a track around the wood line gathering timber. She sat, trying to light a fire with her frustration building with every strike of the two rocks. She wished she paid more attention to girl scouts during fire-making lessons instead of pining over Nancy Tubermaker.

The soft, timid voice sprung from the darkness behind her, and Raven spun around. "Can I help you with that?" Peggy asked.

"That would be nice. Join me." Raven scooted over on the log.

Peggy stepped over with one foot at a time. She plopped down, giving a soft smile with embarrassment about how hard she hit the timber. She snapped her two fingers, and the fire roared upwards. Huge flames reached to the sky before settling back down to a flicker.

"Wow. That's impressive." Raven said.

"Thanks. It's nothing." Peggy responded.

"So, what's your story? I hope that wasn't too

blunt. I'm sorry, but seeing fairies is one in a million. Plus, your magic is mind-blowing." Raven stared at the woman sitting next to her. She was beautiful — nothing like the dirty, matted hair little girl that they met. Her features were kind. Small freckles covered her nose. The once matted hair was long, straight, and laid down her back, touching the tip of her butt. Her eyes were spellbinding.

Peggy smiled. "I understand that you could be nervous about being around me. I mean neither you nor Brandy Lee any harm." Peggy inhaled. "My frollick was traveling when a sudden wind blew us into the lake. Some of us died. Then she showed up — the witch. We were still trying to recover from the fall and the deaths of our loved ones. She didn't appear in her form but of a mother fairy. We trusted her to help us. She took us in, and we slept with comfort for the night. We were to leave the next day. During our sleep, she cast a spell turning us into children, suppressing all our powers. It was a brilliant scheme, considering all the magic and power a family of fairies contains. We could've crushed her." Peggy stared into the fire. For a moment, her words stopped before they started again. "Years we were trapped. Theo and Red bullied us all. Before we knew it, they were working with the witch. I had caused trouble throughout the years, and wanted to kill her. They banished me from the group. It was hard to fight them all." Sadness filled her words, and Raven was finding grief filling her heart for the lost woman.

Raven remembered from her studies that fairies are born to a family. They travel in frollicks. They need them to survive, or loneliness will slowly kill them. It ran across her thoughts: *What was in store for the lost fairy?* "Thank you for helping us back there. I know you went against your family."

"I lost my family a long time ago. Heartbreak fills me. Everyone wasn't bad, and I miss my friends. We remained under control with Theo and Red's fear tactics. They were terrible fairies." Peggy twisted her wrist, and the fire blazed. She felt an arm wrap around her shoulder in comfort, as eyes stared into the flames. "Your turn. What's up with you and Brandy Lee? You're not trying to find a friend. So, why in the world are a vampire and a she-wolf tracing around the Dark Forest?"

Figuring it was a gamble, Raven told her the whole story about Brandy Lee. The royal family and the kill order part. She explained the attempt to kill Brandy Lee by an elder. They were traveling to the council of she-wolves for answers, hoping the kill order could get canceled and the question answered. Was Brandy Lee part of the royal family?

Peggy listens with intensity. Once Raven's words faded to a stop, Peggy spoke. "The royal family has not existed for centuries. Hard to believe an heir lives in these times, but I guess it might be possible."

"Would you want to help us reach the council? I know it may be a lot to ask, but your magic is irreplaceable."

Peggy thought about her choices. Leave the forest and get lost in a big world alone with no friends. Loneliness. The kryptonite of fairies. Or, stay with these two new women and face the woods and evil. She owed a debt. She owed her freedom to them. The answer already decided before the question got asked. She would help the two move forward.

"No need to ask. I'll help you." Peggy answered, knowing they were helping her also. Alone in these woods would be a death sentence for a single fairy.

Other than the kiss in the tent, Raven smiled again with a tingle of hope in her heart. Both tired, she didn't want to dig for any more details. Raven inhaled, and with a massive burst of air whisking from her, she blew the fire out in one puff. With a smirk, "I have a little magic too."

"I see. Nice." Peggy stood. Raven stood.

"Let's go get some rest. I can feel the sun minutes away. Thank you again, Peggy, for saving us."

"Ditto, Raven."

After a long embrace, they headed towards the tent. Peggy stopped in her tracks, allowing Raven to enter first. Raven turned to find the young girl twirling her hands in circles. The ground lifted and tossed around them. A dome grew over them made of the dirt, leaves, and branches. Standing sturdy and tall, it turned the tiny tent into a fortress. Dipping her head, Peggy entered the tent, and the wall closed. “Safer for us.” She whispered before zipping up the tent.

Tomorrow will bring a new night, but now, they would sleep.

16
Bacon Bacon

Stretching her arms, Brandy Lee rolled to her back, feeling refreshed and rejuvenated. She lifted her head and glanced around the tent. Peggy wasn't inside. Raven's body laid spread out beside her, still asleep. The beauty of the woman drew her attention like a magnet. She rolled over, propping herself up on one elbow. "God, you are gorgeous," she whispered. Her long black hair cascaded down the front of her. She laid on her back with her arms crossed across her chest. Brandy Lee smiled. Raven looked like the typical vampire in the movies. Her pale skin perfect. Kissable lips teased at a distance.

"Why are you smiling?" Raven whispered in a sleepy voice.

"Because of you." Brandy Lee responded.

Fingers slipped along the side of her face, wrapping around the back of her neck. Brandy Lee felt her body pull down. The kiss so hot, breaths became stolen. Little moans escaped into the tight space. Brandy Lee slid on top. Raven's breath hitched.

"What're you doing?" The words came hard. Raven's mind couldn't focus. Their skin touched under the sheets firing up her nerves. Even with the tee-shirt and underwear between them, Raven could feel her warmth against her cold skin.

"I'm not sure. Show me." Brandy Lee's husky voice filled with passion.

Tingles darted over the skin. Raven let her hands run under her shirt, with nails scratching over the surface of her flesh. Their kiss deepened. Raven felt fingers at the edge of her shirt, and she stopped the kiss. She froze. Raven reached down, grabbing Brandy Lee's hand in an effort to prevent her from going any farther. "No, not here. It's your first time. You deserve better."

Brandy Lee lifted to find those emerald eyes. "I'm where I want to be, here with you. Do you want me because I want you?"

Her words. So naïve, but yet, sexy. "Yes," Raven mustered out the single word. Her body ached for the beautiful blonde. Her nerves on edge, knowing she was a virgin.

As if she heard her thoughts, "Then show me

how to please you."

Raven released the hand that she still grasped. She guided it under her shirt until it scooped up her breasts. Their eyes locked until Raven's grew heavy at a pull of her nipple. Raven's hand fell to Brandy Lee's ass. She pulled at the underwear. "Take these off." Raven felt Brandy Lee pulling and tugging at the underwear. Raven shimmied her panties down. The two articles joined each other at the end of the bed. Raven rolled until she was on top and in control.

"You sure?" Raven asked one more time. A smear of wetness laid on her thigh from Brandy Lee's center, and she knew the answer before asking. Brandy Lee took her into a kiss to confirm.

Fingers crawled up Brandy Lee's thigh, sending the sexy blonde into a fit of shivers. Raven broke the kiss when she reached her folds. She was so wet. Heavy breaths laid between them. Raven entered, warmth smothering her finger. She watched as Brandy Lee's golden eyes glazed over in desire before transforming into needs. A stroke over her clit and Brandy Lee growled deep from the back of her throat. An uncontrollable moan released from Raven in response. Her own clit throbbed for release. The finger slipped out in slow motion. Raven slipped her body on top. Swollen clits touched. Gasping breaths filled the air. The friction on their nipples intense from the tee-shirts that remained on during their lovemaking. They grinded in rhythm. Raven buried her face deep into the sexy neck. The pulsating artery told her Brandy Lee was close. She slipped her lips to her ear, whispering, "Please. Come for me." Raven felt the body under her tense and shudder. Fingernails dug deep into her back just as Brandy Lee released. Raven followed her with her explosion. They collapsed with heavy breaths.

"You're quiet. Is everything okay?" Raven asked. Her fingers caressed the back of the tousled blonde hair. Raven enjoyed the woman in her arms.

"I'm perfect." She gave a squeeze around her waist. "It was perfect." With a lift of the head, a soft kiss whispered across Raven's lips. "You're perfect." The words seeped out between the kiss. Brandy Lee's nose wrinkled. She sniffed. "Is that bacon? I smell bacon!" She stiff-armed off Raven.

Raven giggled. "Are you hungry?"

"Starved." Brandy Lee said. A she-wolf's metabolism is high, and food intake is a must, unlike a vampire that can go days without substance. She kissed Raven's cheek and started to search for her underwear.

Raven laughed.

"What?" Brandy Lee asked, trying to turn her underwear from inside out. She twisted it a few times before the article ended up the right way.

"Nothing. You're cute, that is all." Raven released an inner laugh as she thought. *I just got dumped like a one-night stand for bacon. Meat of all things.* She started the search for her underwear.

Peggy sat at the fire, stirring something in a homemade pan that would pop at her. Each jump from the surprise pop received a small child's giggle in response. Her voice sang out a sweet tune with the words unfamiliar to the English language. Small animals ventured from the forest to listen to her. Chipmunks, squirrels, deer, and birds sat looking with their heads bobbing up and down in rhythm as the young girl serenaded them.

Raven and Brandy Lee soon stepped from the tent after finding all their pieces of clothing. Raven's arm touched Brandy Lee's upper arm, stopping her in place. She pointed to all the animals that circled the fairy. They swayed to the music. "That's amazing," Raven whispered. They continued to walk over towards the sweet smell and Peggy. Her back was to them. A few animals darted away in fear of the two strangers that were interrupting the concert. "Good morning, Peggy. You are in a good mood." Raven said, announcing their presence.

With a turn of the head, Peggy smiled ear to ear. “Hi, ladies. Hungry?”

“Yes, but how did you find bacon and a pan out here?” Brandy Lee asked as she sat on the log.

“Magic.” Peggy's words came out with a giggle. “It feels so good to be me again. Thank you for freeing me.”

“We owe you a thank you also. We may have been in a witch’s soup if not for you.”

Raven broke into the conversation. “I’m going to scope the area. Be back soon. Then we can get going.”

“Are you not hungry?” Brandy Lee asked.

“Not really. I will grab a bag of blood. Enjoy the food that Peggy prepared. I’ll be back soon.”

“I don’t like that you are going off by yourself.” Brandy Lee said.

“I won’t go far. I will be within an ear shouting distance.”

“Seriously? You know how far I can hear?”

“Exactly.” Raven gave a cocky smile. “I promise I’ll be safe.” Raven took off, running towards the shadows.

Brandy Lee took the full plate. At least a pound of bacon and eggs teased her nostrils. Peggy sat down beside Brandy Lee on the log with her plate. Their eyes moved from one plate to the other. Laughter rang out between the two of them. Brandy Lee’s plate looked as if she was feeding an army with close to triple the amount.

"You're gorgeous, Peggy." Brandy Lee said between bites. "Nothing like the child version. Raven caught me up on how the Lake Witch trapped all the fairies. Hard to believe a frollick of fairies got tricked by witchcraft. Are you going to be okay without them?"

Peggy lowered her head and stared at her feet. "I don't know. If I get lonely, I'll die a slow death. But," Her words paused for a moment. A rainbow-colored tear fell down her cheek. "If I die? It's better than being trapped at the lake."

"Well, I will not let that happen." Brandy Lee said. "No loneliness. You have Raven and me."

"Your magic is amazing. I assume that you can fly?"

"Not far without my frollick; maybe a half-mile. My magic is limited to nature, with a few exceptions. Like the frying pan, I made it of wood. But I pulled the metals from the ground to make it fireproof. How I got my hands on bacon and eggs; well, I will keep that secret to myself." Peggy gave a wink.

"Doesn't matter to me the resources, it is delicious." Brandy Lee ate, enjoying every bite with enthusiasm. She shoved the last slice of bacon into her mouth. "Sorry, I know I look like a pig. She-wolves consume a lot of food. Our metabolism is high."

"You look as if you're in great shape. That much food would go straight to my hips and stick like glue." The girls giggled, but they stopped when Raven came in sight.

Raven ran across the small field in enormous strides. Her face was red, and the other two ladies stood up, preparing for the worst news. Was Theo chasing her or the black panther? She drew near the camp, and the red line of blood that dripped down her temple became visible. "Get in the tent." The words struggled to lift over the wind, an odd buzzing sound growing stronger. A large, black towering cloud rose towards the sky, casting a black shadow over the grassy field. It dipped down and gained speed at an alarming rate towards the women.

They tumbled over the log, hitting the ground before their feet pushed them towards the tent. A dive caused them to fall into the middle of the sleeping bags. Raven ran inside, and with a twist, she zipped the tent up just as they got hit with a powerful force, so hard the stakes broke free of the ground. The canvas turned over and over like a tumbleweed, with the ladies twisting and turning inside. The three grunted when the tent slammed against a huge oak tree. The shrilling sound of a swarm of bugs deafened them. They cupped their hands over their ears. Wings fluttered around them as a shrilling drone sound filled the air. Then silence. Lowering their hands, with eyes wide open, they untangled themselves while kicking the contents of the tent off the top of their bodies.

"What the hell was that?" Brandy Lee broke the silence.

"A swarm of cicadas," Raven said as she kicked a pillow away.

Catching Brandy Lee's attention was Peggy, who still laid on the floor of the tent. "Peggy, what's the matter? Are you hurt?"

She was lying on her side, her chest rising and falling at a rapid rate. Her breaths sucked in through her mouth in quick puffs. Fear settled into her eyes as they became fixed on a mysterious space.

"Something is wrong with Peggy." Brandy Lee told Raven.

"Shit. Take slow breaths. Let me look." The unfortunate fairy struggled to gather her air. Wheezing sounded from her mouth with every inhale and pain registering on her face. She took the brunt of the hit, slamming her back into the old oak.

The shirt got lifted slow and gentle as the young girl cried out. Bruised skin over her ribs was a shade of deep purple. Oddly shaped bones laid unevenly under the skin, waiting to break through with a wrong twist. Raven and Brandy Lee's eyes met with no words needed. Raven needed to heal her. Unfortunately, there would be a massive amount of pain.

Her head laid in her lap. Brandy Lee leaned over, whispering in the whimpering girl's ear. "Listen, Peggy. Raven can heal you, but it will hurt." Brandy Lee wiped the tears made of the rainbow colors from her cheek. A stick was placed in Peggy's mouth to control her screams. Suddenly, Peggy started to hum the same song she was singing at breakfast. Brandy Lee nodded for Raven to start.

The emerald color converted to solid whites and hands hovered the broken bones. Raven chanted. A hard push down into the flesh and Peggy bucked. Her humming turned into muffled screams. The body jerked in agony. Brandy Lee felt fingernails dig into her thigh until her skin dented with impressions. Peggy begged for the pain to stop before she passed out. Her body went limp. Raven finished the healing, but not before her own tears flowed. "Let her rest, and then we will leave." Raven and Brandy Lee gathered the disarray of items. Brandy Lee stopped to touch the dried blood on Raven's temple. "It's healed. Fell while I was running and hit my head on a rock." She leaned over and kissed Brandy Lee's cheek. "Let's keep picking up this stuff. I am ready to get going." Unlike the last time when Raven told Brandy Lee she was ready to leave, and Brandy Lee didn't listen to her, this time she would.

17

Gone

They were on an uphill climb. The gym's Stairmaster was a bunny hill compared to a workout placed on the women's thighs. Calf muscles shook under pressure. Peggy led the pack with tiny hands waving back thicket. Each lady grabbed at the prickly vines, trying to find an advantage on the vertical trail. Peggy stopped, turning her head to glance back at the two before yelling, "Tell me why again … why we can't fly up this mountain? I think I can carry us to the top."

A sudden stop caused Brandy Lee to run into the back of Raven. Dismissing the circumstances they were in, the face plant into her butt made her laugh inside. She inhaled, but the stale air only stalled inside her lungs. "Because we are an easy target.

We can't protect ourselves in flight. A few more hundred feet, and we will be at the top."

Peggy turned back to the task at hand. She dug deep and pushed herself on. She felt good after Raven fixed her in the tent. The euphoric feelings earlier were smothered by the climb up Mt. Hell. She parted two small blue fir trees and found flat land. Then, she collapsed. Raven and Brandy fell beside her in a heap. "What's wrong with your two councils? They couldn't be like a high-rise where Uber is more accessible."

Standing, Raven turned in a circle, accessing their situation. The ground was flat for miles, and the forest was not as thick. With only four hours of nighttime, the question: *Should they stop here for the night?* It looked safe, but the lake also looked safe at first glance. The decision to press on was decided upon before it got debated in her head. Raven figured it was another day or two before they would reach the council. Peggy and Brandy Lee sat back to back with their beaten-down bodies using each other as a leaning post.

"Ladies, we need to keep moving." Raven ignored the look that she received from the two women. "Come on, another hour or two and we will stop," Raven promised. She slapped forearms with Peggy, yanking her to her feet. They both turned and pulled Brandy Lee to her feet.

In a rhythm march, Peggy started to sing. "Hi ho,

Hi ho. . ."

Raven and Brandy Lee laughed.

"Are you laughing at me?" Peggy asked.

"No; yes. Do all fairies sing?" Brandy Lee asked.

"Yes, we do. It calms us. Try it with me."

Peggy's voice sang out in the darkness. The pace picked up. Arms swung wildly from front to back, and steps grew two folds. Brandy Lee joined in. Raven shook her head side to side. Reluctantly, she joined in. "Hi ho, hi ho, throughout the forest we go." In a single file, the vampire, she-wolf, and fairy traveled forward. The answers they for which they searched decreased with each stride. Before long, Raven was leading them in the song and down the path.

She stopped dead in her tracks, holding up her hand for the other ladies to a halt. She listened. Something wasn't right. There was a swooshing sound coming from under the ground. Squatting, she placed her hand on the ground and the dirt moved. Yanking her hand back, she stood up. The two other ladies cocked their heads, trying to find the source of the sound. *Swoosh. Swoosh.* Raven looked at Brandy Lee. "What's . ." Her words cut off. The ground opened and swallowed her. She was just there talking, and then she dropped. Her head disappeared beneath the soil in a flash.

"Raven!" Brandy Lee screamed her name. Her

body fell to the side of the hole, as her eyes searched. Nothing. It was a hole filled with darkness and no trace of her friend. “Raven!” She screamed again, the name echoing down into the depths of emptiness. She turned her head to look up at Peggy. “Peggy, where’d she go? We need to help her. I am going after her.” Brandy Lee stood, preparing to jump down after the woman she loved. A hand grabbed her.

“No, that is an underground river. The current will suck you in like it did Raven.” Peggy’s eyes squinted in thought. “Come on. The river will surface, and that’s where we can find her. Stay quiet and let me follow the water.” Peggy’s hand grabbed Brandy Lee, pulling her down the path.

Their feet hit the ground at a rapid pace. The river was flowing faster than they could keep up. Stopping every so often, Peggy would circle with her eyes searching for a clue, only to refocus and race off. A clearing laid straight ahead, and Peggy was still pulling Brandy Lee by her wrist. She couldn’t find the words to explain to Brandy Lee that they may not find Raven, at least not alive. The road forked in three different pathways. “Shit,” Peggy said between short breaths. “The river divides.” Her body twisted around. “I don’t know which way to go,” She admitted. Her body came still as the air. Concentration covered her brow. “Fuck. I can’t tell. The water all sounds the same.”

"Just pick one." Brandy Lee pleaded. The tears held back behind fear-filled eyes.

Peggy chose the middle one. Neither one is a better choice than the other. She split her decision, taking the middle path. A few steps into the dirt path, and it got proven that her decision was a mistake.

The black blur fell from the tallest tree, landing on all fours. A low snarl from the back of the cat's throat released, and the two girls froze in their tracks. The cat hunched low to the ground, ready to jump in a snap. A gentle sway of the tail with her massive paws dug into the dirt, leaving deep indentions of her footprint. Black eyes stared before her tongue licked at her lips, as if she was about to devour a two-course meal. Their trail was blocked by the colossal cat. She growled again, more profound than the last.

Brandy Lee now reversed the wrist hold and pulled Peggy backward into her space. "Let's try another way." Brandy Lee said. She could change and fight the advisory, but that didn't seem to be the best choice. They needed to find Raven, who was fighting for her life.

A shift on their heels and they gravitated towards the path to the left of the cat. They felt the cat's eyes following them. The panther pushed off the muscular back legs, hurdling the bushes to land in their passageway. Peggy felt a wave of anger creep through her veins.

Peggy murmured through clench teeth. "I am about to toss a fireball at her." Before she could lift her arms to send the missile of flames, her movements were stopped by Brandy Lee's words.

"No, don't hurt her. Let's try the latter path. Just back up with me." Brandy Lee was already stepping in reverse. Peggy followed.

Stepping into the third and last split in the road, the ladies looked over and noticed the panther laid on the ground. There was no effort in a chase. Her body was sprawled out, as she licked her front paw with lazy eyes. In a jog, they took off.

Stopping a reasonable distance from the threat of the cat, Brandy Lee halted in the middle of the path. Tears filled her eyes, as she paced back and forth. Her breathing was coming in small gasps. The thought of Raven lost under the ground, or even worst, the fact she was dead, overwhelmed her. She bent at the waist, her head hovering over her knees. Cries released.

"Take a breath for me," Peggy asked as she rubbed the young girl's back. "There's always a chance she survived."

Brandy Lee tossed her blonde hair back, running her hands through it before rubbing at her eyes. "She isn't dead. She isn't. She'll find me. But . . ." Brandy Lee paused, swallowed hard. "The sun's almost up." Her voice cracked. She turned her head upwards, the warmth hitting her chin. The knot in her stomach grew. Tears rolled in a steady stream down her cheek.

"She'll protect herself from the sun. She's smart. Let's make camp. We're both sleepy, and Raven'll look for us as soon as the sun goes down. We need to be strong."

What Peggy said was true. At least, Brandy Lee needed to believe that. She just found Raven, and the thought of losing her tore her heart into pieces. Growing up in foster care, she learned not to trust, and it was hard to let your guard down. Raven was the first person who she allowed inside her heart.

The tent popped up in minutes, and Peggy surrounded their sleeping quarters with an extra shield. Just in case, the black panther made another appearance. The two ladies laid next to each other, listening to the animals outside in the forest. The world came to life as the sun rose in the sky. Brandy Lee focused on a stained spot on the top of the tent. Her mind became overfilled in thought.

"We'll find her," Peggy whispered. Her eyes half closed, sleep threatened her. "Can I ask you why you didn't want me to throw a fireball at the cat? I could've crushed her."

Brandy Lee's eyes didn't move from the spot from which she stared on the top of the tent. "I don't know. There was a connection to her. I can't explain it, but it felt like the right thing to do."

"Hmmm…" The last thing heard before Peggy dozed off.

Brandy Lee rolled over to her side, staining her pillow with tears. She thought about Raven and home. What was going on at home? She missed Lady Rochelle.

18
At Home

She gasped as the last bit of orgasm left her body. Collapsing on top of the beautiful redhead below her, she listened as the brunette lying on her ass released herself. Lady Rochelle rolled off the woman underneath her. They climaxed together, taking each other to the limits. Followed by hearing the third lady explode seconds later, it topped off the ménage à trois. Both the redhead and brunette snuggled into their leader and lover's arms.

A knock on the door ended the sexual bliss Lady Rochelle relished. "Enter," She announced. The two women pulled a sheet over their leader before snuggling naked in her arms. Lady Rochelle took notice, making a mental note to award both later for their loyalty and sexual boldness.

"I'm sorry, my Lady. Your sister wishes to enter." The older woman announced.

Before Rochelle could answer the request, her sister Queen Lana pushed past the older woman and stood at the foot of Rochelle's bed. She took notice of the delicious sight wrapped in her sister's arms. Under any other circumstances, Lana would try to think of ways to seduce the women, enticing them for maybe a second round with her. Lana pushed past the thoughts and the smear of jealously which peaked at her sister's slice of heaven.

Her face became serious. "Dismiss your toys so we can talk." She ordered.

The look on Rochelle's face was not of agreement. She gave her sister a raised eyebrow in disapproval. Frowning, she considered whether the sudden intrusion into her bedroom could be about Brandy Lee and Raven arriving at the She-Wolf Council, or worse, her getting the news that they were dead. Whatever the reason, Rochelle knew playtime was over. Soft kisses lingered on each of the women's heads, before she dismissed the gorgeous creatures. Both naked women passed by Lana, their fingers tracing across her biceps. This earned a glance back as the perfect asses strolled away.

"Nice taste, Sis," Lana said before she turning her head back toward her sister.

Rochelle was tying up the white robe. "Thank

you. They're a pleasure." Tying her long hair up in a ponytail before twisting it up on the top of her head in a bun, she poured herself a glass of whiskey. "You want one?" She offered.

"No, thanks," Lana answered.

Rochelle turned, leaning against the bar on one elbow. "Okay, so why are you barging in my bedroom in the early night with your panties all bunched up?"

"My tribe is in an uproar. Vampires want Brandy Lee brought to our courts and sentenced."

"Sentenced for what? The young girl hasn't broken any laws." Rochelle brought the glass to her lips and thought before taking a sip. "My Pack won't tolerate your Tribe placing one of ours on trial in a court of vampires." Her eyes closed as she drank the brown liquid. "Ridiculous."

Lana sat down on the lounge, crossing her legs at the ankles. "Exactly. There are reports that fights are breaking out in local areas between my vampires and your she-wolves. No killings yet, but there will be a riot if that occurs. We'll lose control of our people."

This news did not sit well with Rochelle, and she tried to understand the thoughts of others. If it was real and Brandy Lee was royalty, it would terrify vampires. As a result, the world would return to the ancient days. The she-wolf royalty family reigned over all vampires and humans many years ago. It took a civil war and many centuries for the vampires to rise. The fear of returning to those days fed the fear.

"I questioned some of my vamps and found out there is a bounty on Brandy Lee's head. Dead or alive. That is why there were attempts on her life."

Rochelle took a deep breath. "Any word from them? Do we know if they reached the council?"

Lana shook her head, wishing deep down inside that alcohol affected her. She needed to be numb. Not knowing drove her crazy. They should have reached the councils by now, and the Empress of the Vampires, Katherine, should have contacted Lana. Supposedly, it was rogue vampires that placed the bounty instead of the council. If the highest of wolves recognize Brandy Lee as a royal, and the vampire council stops the bounty, the mayhem may cease.

"Lana, you okay? You are in deep concentration." Rochelle's words rang out.

"I am fine. Was thinking that, if the girls have reached the council by now, Empress Katherine should have contacted me."

Rochelle nodded in agreement. "Brandy Lee still has to prove to the She-Wolf Council she is of the royal family. There will be a test. That night we were together with Brandy Lee and Raven. You noticed the odd smell. Didn't you?"

"What odd smell?" Lana stood and walked over

to the bar, pouring herself a drink. It wouldn't ease the tension that radiated between her shoulders, but she could pretend.

"Don't play dumb, Sis. It doesn't become you. You smelled the same thing I did that night. Something was off in the odor of her blood."

Lana listened to her sister, knowing about what she spoke of that night was real. She didn't want to talk about it. She released a puff of air.

"Damnit, Lana! When did you become such a wimpy ass?"

Lana hissed with her fangs gleaming. Rochelle responded with a low growl from the back of her throat. They stared each other down, daring the other to blink. Rochelle broke the eye hold.

"Why are we fighting amongst ourselves?" Rochelle asked.

Lana lowered her eyes. "I smelled it. Something is off. The royal blood was strong, but there was a small mixture of something in it. The slightest hint of something else teased my nostrils. I chalked it up as an odor lingering in the air."

"We know that was not it. I hope we didn't sentence Brandy Lee and Raven to death, sending them to the councils." Rochelle undid the robe and retied the sash. "So, how do we stop our people from fighting?" She took a long draw off the brown liquid. "If one of your vampires kills one of my Pack, the wolves will rip apart any vampire they see on the streets. We need to heed the outcome and pray it gets fixed by the council."

"You said it. Death. That's the answer. We can announce that Brandy Lee has died. Make a fake shrine and have a fake funeral. That will bide us some time."

Rochelle nodded. "Yes, that may work. I will prepare the announcement. Let's hope it isn't much longer before we hear from them."

The sister's clinked their glasses together. "To family and peace."

19
You Again

Emerging from the tent, Brandy Lee rose upon her tiptoes, her arms stretched above her head. She looks for Raven until yesterday's events flash through her thoughts, but then she realized Raven was still missing. A shiver runs through her body. Was it from her loss of Raven or the temperature? It didn't matter. Her arms wrapped around herself for warmth. A moment thought of fleeing home to Lady Rochelle filled her mind. She would protect her; help her hide. Before her life went to hell, all she wanted to do was make her leader proud of her and be a good driver. Now, she was fighting her way through woods filled with evil and trying to get to a council she doesn't know. What if the vampire council tried to kill her? On top of everything else, the woman with who she was falling in love might be dead. It is too much for a twenty-two-year-old.

A noise came from the trees behind her, and she spun. The leaves rustled before Peggy, who stepped from the bushes with her arms full. “Hey! Good evening. You were tired. I noticed you were sleeping like a rock.” Peggy said, moving towards some stones set in a circle. She dropped the armload of wood that she carried inside the tent, rocks twisting her wrist. A fire roared up. “Isn’t that a crazy saying?”

Brandy Lee joined her. She held her hands out, warming the digits. “Crazy saying?”

“Sleeping like a rock. Rocks don’t sleep.” Peggy said.

“I guess it is.” Brandy Lee said with distance in her voice. “Is it colder this evening?”

“Yes, it is. I noticed it too. Are you hungry? I can make some food.”

Brandy Lee stared into the fire. Her appetite was not as hefty as usual. A sick feeling filled her stomach. “No, not really.” She responded.

“Eat, because you need strength; and then we need to get going.” A shiver ran through Peggy’s body. The cold was visible by the goosebumps forming patterns on her arms.

“You are freezing.” Brandy Lee said as a statement rather than a question. She watched the thin girl nod her head.

"Listen. I'll run around the area. Maybe there'll be a sign of the underground river, or even better, a sign of Raven. Maybe I can find something to keep you warm, but until then, there is a long-sleeved flannel shirt in Raven's bag. I saw her wear it the other day. Fix me something to eat, and we can get going. Deal?"

"Deal," The fairy said through chattering teeth. "Don't take too long." Peggy requested.

"I won't. And thank you for your help. Be back soon. Get some clothes on those arms." Once again, a nod followed to confirm Brandy Lee's request.

Peggy watched Brandy Lee dart off before she turned towards the tent. Once inside, she searched for the shirt. Finding the article, she placed it on herself and rubbed her arms.

"I've forgotten how beautiful you are." The voice came from behind her.

Peggy froze in place. Closing her eyes, she exhaled without an inhale. Turning around, she came face to face with Theo. "You're making it cold?"

Theo smirked. He stepped back, allowing Peggy to exit the tent. She realized Theo was alone. The frollick was nowhere close. If he were alone this whole time, he would be weaker. "Where's your back-up?" Peggy asked.

"They left me. I protected our frollick all those years, and they left me. Because of you!" The words screamed at her. “It’s you and that hairy wolf’s fault. Oh, and that bloodsucker too.” He moved his eyes side to side, looking for Raven. When he saw no evidence of her presence, he continued. “You ruined everything and killed Red.” His temper raged, and the veins bulged from his forehead. His round glasses sat on the tip of his nose with a broken lens, his hair tousling. Peggy took a step towards him. He raised his hand but then let it fall. The temperature dropped by ten degrees.

Peggy fell to her knees as the chill rushed through her body. The frigid air stung like bees, and she grabbed at the dirt to steady herself.

Theo swirled his arm before dumping water over her. He smiled when Peggy cried out. “Ah, and I thought you like to play with ice.”

“Theo. Please,” Peggy’s pleas fell on deaf ears.

Revenge was his drive, and nothing would deter it. He walked around the shivering wet woman on all fours. He lifted his arm again and dropped them. Once again, the temperature dropped another ten degrees.

Her breath puffed from her in a cloud. A thousand needles shot through her veins. She collapsed in a fetal position and prepared for death. Her muscles were so heavy that she couldn’t lift them. Uncontrollable shivers ravished her body. Icicles hung from frozen strands of hair. Unable to lift her head, she closed her eyes and said a private prayer.

The breath warmed her ear before the words. Theo leaned close. “Don’t worry, my friend. I won’t kill you, just yet. I want your friends to watch.” Theo leaned back on his heels. “Where’s your friends?” He looked around, rotating his shoulders left then right.

“Raven is dead, and Brandy Lee ran off. I am alone.” The words were barely audible.

Theo waved his hand over the dying body, and warmth smothered her like a blanket. Her body still encased by cold, but the heat rose around her. Peggy took a deep breath into her lungs. She came up to her knees. “Please, Theo; let’s leave. You can’t be alone, or death will be slow for you.”

He leaned back on his heels, and belly laughed. His shoulders jiggled as he chuckled out, “I died when my wife died in the lake and then again when you killed Red.”

Peggy figured Theo was crazy mad. She was the one choked by Red, and it was him that hit her upside the head with the rock. Mentioning this would not help, so she bit her lower lip. Her eyes searched around for Brandy Lee. Peggy’s screams should have been loud enough to have Brandy Lee running to help. Where was she? Did Theo capture her or maybe the black panther? Peggy shook her head from side to side as she tried to erase the negative thoughts.

The laughter stopped, and Theo looked around. His eyes searched for something. When he found that for which he was looking, he smiled. Twisting his body from the waist up, he reached out. With magic, he pulled the roots from the trees towards him. Breaking free from the soil, they twisted and turned like snakes slithering across the ground before wrapping around Peggy's wrists and ankles. They tightened and bound her to the earth. She fell back to the ground, locking her body in place. She struggled to no avail. The roots were strong as chains, and she was now a prisoner at the hands of Theo.

"You look hot spread out like that, Peggy. A big difference from that matted, dirty girl that was a pain in my ass." Theo sat down on the log. "Let's wait for that dog. Shall we?"

"Fuck you!" Peggy yelled as she pulled at the vines.

The hit came hard from the rear; Theo's glasses flew across the grass. He tumbled over, hitting the dirt with a thump. The white wolf's body came to a stop yards away. With a slow turn, she crept back towards Theo, a snarl across her face with white teeth clenched. Theo struggled to gain his footing. He saw the white wolf leap and so he countered the assault. A ball of wind slammed into Brandy Lee, knocking her to the ground. A whimper released as her body hit the dirt. That same smirk crossed his lips.

Peggy twisted her wrist, trying to get released, but the vines sliced into her flesh as rainbow blood dripped from her. Colors of the spectrum seeped from her veins and overtook the brown earth. With soil shuffling under her hand, she twisted her head and watched small, pointy green stems wiggle from the depths. The thorns were sharp as razors. Her attention ripped from the beauty of growth when Brandy Lee's wail of pain pierced her ears.

He stood above her, twisting his wrist into figure eights, orchestrating the vines that encased the wolf's body. The vines cut her like barbed wire turning her white fur scarlet. His enjoyment reached a climax with every cry of agony. He would kill her and find pleasure in every minute.

Peggy jerked her attention back to the flower blooming from her blood. Stretching her wrist towards the small bud, she rubbed the rope of vine across the sharp piece of the stem. It tore with ease under the blade. Her right wrist became loose, and she reached over to untie her left. Time was running out. She frantically pulled at the vine.

"Damn!" She screamed. She lifted her head to watch Theo tightened the squeeze on her friend, laughing.

As it dropped from the sky, the panther pounced onto Theo, digging her teeth into his throat. Blood covered the front of his white shirt in a flash flood of red. Opening her jaws, she bit down again between his neck and arm. A vice grip of teeth sunk deep into his skin. Theo's cry of pain echoed so loud through the trees that it caused birds to fly from the treetops. The panther dragged him kicking and screaming into the woods as the thickness of the dark forest swallowed them. Theo's scream faded in the distance until the air once again became silent.

Brandy Lee laid still in the distance, laying in a heaping pool of blood. Peggy pulled at the vines holding her. Reaching her last knot, she unraveled the thickness wrapped around her ankles. The air warmed around her. Theo was dead, therefore his magic ended. Crawling over to her, Peggy tore the roots from the ground, releasing Brandy Lee from their grasp. Not sure where to touch the wolf, she rubbed her head. She watched as the deep gashes began to heal, closing at a rapid rate. Peggy blew a sigh of relief. She was glad Brandy Lee could self-heal. She continued to rub her head until the wolf came to a sitting position. Her golden eyes searched the perimeter for Theo.

"The panther took him. Theo is dead." Peggy told the panting wolf.

Brandy Lee changed, her naked human body showed no signs of the torture. Peggy took off the flannel shirt she still wore and put it around the bare woman. A smile thanked her, and a hand covered hers in gratitude.

"Did he hurt you?" Brandy Lee asked.

"No, nothing permanent," Peggy responded.

"What happened to him? I must've passed out. I remember very little."

"That black panther jumped out from nowhere, dragging him into the forest. He was causing the cold, and when the temperature came back to normal, the vines stopped twisting. I knew he was dead. His magic was wasted on evil."

"Are we ever going to get a break?" Since the day they left, it was one challenge after the other.

A low groan rumbled from under the bush, causing both ladies to stand back up. Brandy Lee prepared to change back into her wolf form. If the black panther showed, she would give her a fight. The sound, more than a moan this time, had Brandy Lee reaching into her backpack. She broke the yellow vial of blood and downed the liquid. She was tired; the change had drained her. The red liquid slid down her throat, and the blood ran through her heart. She stood tall when the faint sound of a name called to her.

"Bran . . ." the low voice mumbled, hidden by the breeze.

"Did you hear that?" Brandy Lee asked as she crept towards a set of bushes.

"Hey, that might be Theo. Be careful." Peggy said to the curious woman.

She turned her head back at Peggy. "You said he was dead, and the cat isn't calling my name." Her head still turned to talk when a hand grabbed her ankle. Brandy Lee screamed as the charred hand grasped at her ankle. Skin hung off the fingers in long strands exposing the white bone. Brandy Lee's eyes widened as they followed the arm into the bushes. The leaves separated, and a burned face emerged into the moonlight, begging for help.

"Peggy. It's Raven!" Brandy Lee exclaimed.

20

Don't Die

She fell into darkness . . .

Pain tore through every nerve ending. She wanted to die a quick, painless death. It would be a wishful blessing compared to the current suffering placed on her. Raven traveled down the underground river after the endless drop into the deep hole. Her body tossed like a rag doll in a small cramped space, with her skin torn by submerged rocks and branches. Her bones were broken into pieces by the earth that encased her. Becoming entangled in debris along the way, with scarce air, she broke free and continued down the dark canal. Her body surfaced two miles away. The last thing she remembered was her head hitting a rock, and the world went black.

Something smelt funny. Raven twitched her nose at the smell that jarred her senses back to life, the smell of burning flesh. Her flesh. The left arm burned until the skin hung off the bones in clumps. A huge hole was in the side of her jaw, revealing her teeth. Her left eye moved in an open space. The back of the eye exposed, one could see the entire eye rotate in the socket. She was a two-face vampire — the beautiful Raven on the right and a horrible skeleton on the left. Her final resting place was on a muddy bank on the river, face down with the left side exposed — minimal sun coverage. The pain of her flesh burning jolted her from an unconscious state, her eyes widening before she thrashed around in agony. Scrambling hand over hand onto her belly in the water, her tears mixed with the freshwater. Her mind raced while holding her breath to the last moment. With the previous bit of air gone, she had no choice; she had to surface. She popped her head over the waterline, inhaling between the screams as her face blistered. Raven dipped down under again, but she couldn't keep this up for another twelve hours of daylight.

As she came up for air this time, she dove and gulped a breath of air before she went back under the water. The sun melted the back of her head, but that didn't hurt as bad as her face. Searching under the water, she looked for anything to cover her skin. Long grass waved with the current on the river bottom. Raven pulled some large pieces away, wrapping her arms in the seaweed grass. The cooling sensation relived the pain from her charred skin. A few more diving attempts and most of her body was wrapped in this miracle grass. Memorizing the layout of the river with each dive, she concluded that getting back in the hole would be a challenge. The current was too strong. Greenage caught her eye at the edge of the water. It was a bush that hung over the water. She swam underwater until reaching the low-hanging branches. Coming to the surface, she breathed in the air. The air stung her lungs, but she wasn't on fire. She grabbed the branch and floated underneath.

"Please, help me," She pleaded.

Raven's entire body ached by the time the moon shone over the river. She healed the bones but was too weak to fix the burns. Half her face was gone, and her whole left hand was bones. She needed blood. Swimming to the other side of the river, she crawled her way through the mud. Raven's leg, damaged with her pants, scorched into the back of her leg. She was unable to stand. She started to claw her way through the brush.

An hour later and Raven only managed a quarter of a mile. Creeping at such a slow pace over limbs and branches became an impossible mission. She thought about Brandy Lee being alone and how she fell in love with the woman. Memories surfaced of the sweet taste of her lips. Moans so delicious that they drove her over the edge and into an explosive orgasm. The thoughts of their first time eased the pain. Her mind shifted to her mentor, Queen Lana. How she wished she had studied harder under her. She was a second mother figure to her, and an essential person in her life. Her short life.

Raven's body collapsed. The world faded to gray. She fought the unconscious state that loomed close by, but it was too much. Her vision became blurred, her lips dry. She rolled over to her back. Something black hovered over her. Fear beat in her heart. This was it. She was going to die. The blur that filled her vision was about to eat her for dinner, and she was the main course. A bear? A panther? It didn't matter. She prepared herself for the end.

Something grabbed at her shirt, and then she felt her body be dragged over stumps and roots. She tried to look back at the massive animal pulling her through the woods, but she couldn't see past her nose. Maybe baby bear cubs were waiting for her arrival so they could devour her body in the luxury of their den. In and out of reality, with groans escaping during the conscious moments, she looked up at the trees catching glimpses of the moon.

Her body dumped in some bushes like unwanted trash. Her eyes closed tight, waiting for the kill. Nothing. The animal that dragged her over a mile through the woods was gone. She inhaled a breath.

She coughed, and blood filled her mouth. *That can't be good!* She thought.

Time escaped her as she rolled over, landing face first in the dirt. She groaned in pain and could hear voices close by. Her ears could neither tell who was speaking nor the words, but she could make out the sound of women talking. Maybe, Brandy Lee. She mustered all her strength and yelled. "Bran . . ." before the dryness in her throat strangled her words. *Fuck! Come on, Raven! This may be your only chance.* The thoughts yelled at her. *Get up, Bitch!* Another inside scream.

She mustered all her strength, pushing up on one knee. She reached, finding an ankle. Her burned fingers wrapped around and squeezed with all her might. Her head pushed through the bushes to see the most beautiful golden eyes staring down at her. *Brandy Lee.* The fear in the young girl's eyes told it all. She looked like a monster.

21
Just Breathe

"I can't stop the bleeding," Brandy Lee replaced the red-stained cloth with a fresh white one. Blood seeped from the gaping holes. "Raven, look at me. How do I help you?" She watched as the scared woman's eyes fluttered open.

"Blood." The one word whispered out. Raven's backpack was lost in the underground current, along with the remaining bags of blood.

"No. No. Open your eyes. Peggy, we need blood. Give me my bag." Brandy Lee searched through her bag, finding the red vial of blood. She broke it over Raven's lips.

Raven kept her eyes closed, but she drank the blood with earnest. The two ladies waited to see if there was a change. Raven stayed the same. No strength gained. No healing. Nothing.

"Isn't that wolf's blood? She needs human, a pure animal, or another vampire." Peggy said.

"What about your blood?" Brandy Lee asked in hope.

"No. My blood will kill her. Maybe we can find an animal. I will go look outside." Just as she unzipped the tent, thunder roared across the sky. Lightning slammed into the ground, inches from the tent. "What the hell?" She exclaimed as she fell back on her butt.

Brandy Lee turned her head back to see a storm brewing on the horizon. Everything was pitch black. There was no way they could find any animals in that storm. A moan brought her attention back to Raven.

Her skin was the color of bleach. Gurgles emerged from the back of her throat, her chest rising and falling with each labored breath. Then she stopped. Silence. No gurgling; no breaths. Silence. The blood stopped running through her heart. Raven was dead.

"Nooo!" Brandy Lee screamed. She came to her knees and started pumping Raven's chest. She counted out loud with each thrust down. "One, two, three . . . Thirty!" She breathed into her mouth. She repeated. "One, two, three . . . Thirty!" She breathed into her mouth twice again. Her hands pumped hard. "You are not finding your way back to me, only to die. Start your heart back up." Brandy Lee felt a hand on her upper arm. She shrugged her shoulder, pushing it away. There was no stopping until Raven's heart was beating on its own again. A breath passed from Brandy Lee's mouth into Raven's, and it happens. Raven arched her back and inhaled deeply. She was alive.

The raging storm blew the sides of the tent relentlessly. The bottom felt like it was lifting with each gust. It sounded like a train was coming through the campground with the loud whistle blowing like it was on full throttle. In the distance, the branches cracked under the wind pressure. The trees uprooted, slamming to the ground and causing the earth to shake. If one toppled on the tent, well, there was no time to think about that.

With a massive twirl, the wind unzipped the front of the tent. Peggy struggled to her feet while Brandy Lee fell atop of Raven for protection. In a fight for her life, Peggy pulled down hard on the zipper. The wind was putting up a significant front of resistance. One hard last yank and the tent closed. Peggy sat there on her knees, her head lowered in a state of exhaustion.

Brandy Lee raised off Raven to find her looking up at her. "Hey there. Welcome back."

"Hi," Weakness in her words evident. "I'm thirsty."

Brandy Lee touched the side of her face that remained healthy. The decision got made before she asked herself the question. It won't change her condition. It would quench her thirst but not heal her. She wanted Raven to drink from her.

Slipping her fingers around the back of Raven's head, she lifted her head and placed her arm to her mouth. "Drink, my love." The look she received from Raven was one of confusion and fear. Brandy Lee repeated her words. "Drink. It is okay."

Raven's fangs extended and dug into the flesh. She drained the red liquid. Pressing in harder, she fed. It tasted so good, and Raven was having problems controlling her need. A tingle rippled over her skin. The feeling grew stronger as she filled her belly with the sweet nectar. Her fingers stung as nerves connected back together. Raven was healing slowly, and she was recovering.

The woman she loved was feeding on her. The blood dripped down the sides of her lips. She was so eager it was erotic. A sensation settled in her center, and Brandy Lee moaned. With eyes closed, her fingers tangled in Raven's hair as she struggled to hold Raven's head up. Brandy Lee closed her eyes tighter. Whatever Raven was doing to her felt good. She bit her lip, but it didn't help. Jesus. About to come, she tossed her head back. She didn't scream her climax; it was silent. Waves of electric pulses shot through her body. She came in silence.

Brandy Lee opened her eyes to meet emerald eyes looking at her. Was she being watched? By

Raven or Peggy? A blush crossed her face but disappeared fast. Her jaw dropped open. Raven was healing. The side of her eye enclosed, and the skin repaired to new. Her hand became covered in veins and nerves, connecting like a road map.

"Peggy, come here," Brandy Lee said. "Hold her head up." She pulled her arm away from Raven's mouth. Raven groaned in disagreement. Brandy Lee looked deep into Raven's eyes, and she could see the strength and glow back in her. Pulling her blonde hair to the side, she noticed Raven's eyes widen.

The vampire shook her head.

Brandy Lee leaned over, placing a soft kiss on her cheek. "Yes," A husky voice whispered. She leaned over, and when the fangs pierced her jugular, she released a low growl that vibrated through the tent. Her hands twisted the blankets beneath her to stay upright. It didn't hurt. Once again, it was erotic.

Peggy felt the strength in Raven's neck grow until she could release the hold. Wrapping her hand around Brandy Lee's head, she pulled her closer. With her face buried under the blonde hair, Raven ate. She healed. But at the expense of Brandy Lee, she weakened and collapsed on top of her. Raven pulled away, as fangs retracted from the artery. Her head flung backward, and she screamed. Brandy Lee's blood trailed down the sides of her mouth.

With the face and hand healed, Raven looked anew, refreshed, and stronger than ever before.

Raven picked up Brandy Lee and laid her down. She felt for a pulse. Good. It was strong.

“What’s the matter with her?” Peggy asked, placing a pillow under her head.

“She passed out. Her pulse is strong, but her blood needs to replace itself.” Raven answered.

“Will she be a vampire now?” Another question by Peggy.

“No, we can’t change she-wolves. I took a lot of blood from her. I don’t know how her blood healed me. It’s impossible. A she-wolf’s blood is no good to vampires. It lacks a DNA strand that can heal us or help us get stronger. I don’t understand.”

Peggy looked at the glow radiating from Raven. “Whatever the reason, it changed you. Maybe it’s the royal blood that runs through her, and that’s why you healed from it.”

“I guess.” Raven's attention got pulled back to Brandy Lee when the woman moaned. “Hey, are you waking up for me?”

“Uh-huh,” Brandy Lee murmured. “Why am I so tired?”

“You worked hard at helping me get better. Get some sleep.” Raven snuggled in beside Brandy Lee, spooning her. The storm slowed outside.

Peggy took a quick peek. The sun was only an hour away from rising. “Hey guys, the storm has almost ceased. I will check the surrounding area and make sure no trees will fall on us. Make sure the blank panther left."

Raven lifted her head. "Did you say black panther?"

"Yes, she was here earlier. We got attacked by Theo earlier. I don't know from where the panther came. It was as if she dropped from the sky, but she saved us from Theo. I am sure she was looking for her next meal, but her timing couldn't have been better. Just as we were about to die at the hands of Theo, she attacked him and dragged him into the forest. She killed him."

"Umm, that is odd. A black panther? Something dragged me through the woods and dropped me off in that bush."

"She has shown up at the best times, and she hasn't eaten us yet. We have been lucky. Okay, I'll be back." Peggy said before disappearing out of the flap of the tent.

Raven spooned Brandy Lee again. Soft snores emerged from a tired woman. Raven rubbed her head. "You saved me, Brandy Lee, and not just by your blood. When I was about to give up and die, all I could think of was how I needed to get back to you. You put the drive in my heart." Raven tucked a strand of hair behind the sleeping beauty's ear. "I'm falling in love with you. No, that's a lie. I'm in love with you." Raven laid her head down on her pillow.

"I love you too!" The whisper escaped into the night.

Cuddling closer, Raven smiled.

22
Almost There

Heaviness Heaven.

Raven awoke with the heaviness of a leg draped over her body. An arm laid across her stomach and blonde hair covered her chest. She was in heaven. Is this a dream, or did this beautiful creature tell me she loved me last night? What if she doesn't remember? At this very moment, Raven wished they were back in their hometown of San Francisco sitting by the bay and watching the stars in each other's arms. Oh, but those were daydreams. The truth was that they remained surrounded by a forest, miles from home, and most likely with trouble ahead. Raven sighed.

Brandy Lee stirred. "You okay?"

"Perfect." Raven gave the truthful response.

"Where's Peggy?"

"She went back out again to scope the area. How do you feel?" Raven pushed the hair away from her face.

"You tell me?" Brandy Lee replied in a husky voice.

Raven rolled to her side, her lips inches apart. A hand traced down Brandy Lee's thigh in a gentle touch. Her legs opened, and Raven moaned with pleasure at the giving. "Look at me," Raven ordered. She watched the golden eyes get heavy-lidded, passion turning them to a smoky color. "Don't close your eyes. Watch me." Raven got rewarded with a deep throaty moan.

"Raven, you know I climaxed when you were drinking from my arm."

"Tell me about it." Raven knew the drinking of a vampire was an aphrodisiac. She wanted Brandy Lee to tell her, and she wanted to be in complete control. Her energy level was high. A finger slipped inside the silk panties, rolling her finger up and down the wet folds. "Someone's wet. Now, tell me about that climax."

"It started as a tingle down below, and then it was everywhere. As blood pumped from me, my clit throbbed. So bad that I needed to release."

"Oh, I like that." Raven rolled a finger over her clit, and Brandy Lee gasped. "Is your clit throbbing now?"

"Oh, yes. It is." Brandy Lee closed her eyes as a

wave of wants and needs flooded her.

"Open your eyes." Now, this is the third order coming softer and with a deep rattle. Raven's wetness was already pooling. This woman couldn't be any sexier. "Show me your breasts." Raven sucked in air when the top crept up, and two cherry nipples teased. "Beautiful. I will take the right one in my mouth. Keep your eyes open as I suck. Promise?"

"Yes." Brandy Lee breathed.

Raven flicked her tongue over the nipple while glancing up. She buried her face into the small breast, devouring the nipple. Her teeth scraped it ever so lightly. Brandy Lee pushed her hips into her. Raven pulled back.

"So eager."

"Please."

"Say my name."

"Please, Raven."

"You wanted me to tell you how you feel?"

"Yes, Raven. Tell me."

"You are warm and wet. I can feel your clit throbbing, waiting for me to touch it. You have my finger covered in your juices. Mmm, and your hole is trembling. You want me inside fucking you."

Brandy Lee grasped Raven's upper arm. "Oh, god, please."

"First, this clit. Let me tell you how it feels." Raven rolled her thumb over the hardened bud.

Brandy moaned out. “It’s hard and pulsating.” A more prolonged, louder moan released. “That sounded delicious.” Raven slipped her finger inside. Brandy Lee bucked towards her. “Still eager, I see. You are tight and soft inside.”

“Fuck! I am going to come.”

“Look at me, Brandy Lee. Let me see you come.” Raven picked up a rhythm pace. In and out until she felt the onset of a climax. Her finger sunk deep. Raven watched the woman unravel while she rode her orgasm to the end.

“No more.” Her body spent. Brandy Lee collapsed.

After recovering, Brandy Lee turned the tables and caught Raven off guard. She was on top of her and straddling her stomach. Her wet thighs were slick with juices. Raven’s arousal was at the limit, so, whatever the woman on top of her had in mind, it wouldn’t take much to push her over the edge.

“My turn.” Brandy Lee looked down.

Raven smiled. “I am all yours.”

After their lovemaking, Raven and Brandy Lee fell back asleep. Exhaustion ravaged them from the extra activities, but a familiar voice woke them up.

“You wanna play?” Peggy said with a giggle.

Both ladies lifted their heads, and in unison, their voices rang out. “No.” Remembering the last time Peggy asked them to come out and play, they laughed.

“Then how about some food?” Peggy knew the second question would get more response.

“Now, that’s a yes. We’ll be out in a moment.” Brandy Lee answered for the two of them. “I’m starved.” They watched the brown hair beauty slip out the tent flap.

Raven pulled Brandy Lee into a deep kiss once they were alone again. Passion built. It was Brandy Lee that had the strength to pull away. The hunger roaring in her stomach was overwhelming the desire in her heart. “I’m starving.” The accent placed on each word.

“You’re always starving.” Raven smiled. “I love you.” She whispered.

“I love you. But I love food too.” She smiled.

“Okay, okay. Dumped for a meal again.” They laughed.

The ladies finished the food Peggy prepared, while then packing up the camp. They were looking at a night’s hike before reaching the outskirts of the castle that housed the she-wolves. The plan was to contact the council by the next night, to prove Brandy Lee was an heir of the royal family and then get the kill order removed. It seemed simple, but the ladies knew better than to think it would be anything other than a challenge. First, they hoped they didn't get killed on the spot. Then, there was the council of the vampires. If they found out Brandy Lee is close, or if they were the ones who ordered the kill, then WWIII would break out.

About an hour into the walk, Peggy got quiet. The glow from her skin disappeared beneath worry. She slowed down. Bringing up the rear, she was falling more and more behind. With an arm tug, Brandy Lee stopped Raven in her tracks. She motioned towards Peggy, with her head, who was swatting at a fly. Raven stepped past Brandy Lee. She headed back down the path toward Peggy. Brandy Lee followed.

"Hey, what is going on? You're not singing, and you're falling behind." Raven came to a stop in front of the young girl. "You feel all right?"

Peggy sighed and sat down on a rotten fallen tree. Raven and Brandy Lee joined her, flanking her on both sides. They waited for words, but none came. Peggy placed her face in both of her hands. Tears soon followed, and she felt her cheeks moisten. Heaves of sorrow lifted her shoulders up and down as she started to cry. A hand touched her shoulder.

"Talk to us, Peggy," Brandy Lee asked.

"I'm dying."

Those three words caught the other two women

off guard, their own words at a loss. Brandy Lee leaned over, placing her head on her shoulder. Raven did the same. They sat there in silence. The two women knew loneliness would kill Peggy. Hopes that the companionship with them would be enough fell short. “Tell us how to help.” Brandy Lee's voice rang out.

“You can’t. I need my kind.” Peggy wiped at her eyes. The rainbow tears staining her face, streaks trailing over her skin like war paint. “It’s useless.”

“No, it's not.” The young man’s voice yelled from behind a cluster of trees, startling the girls. Stepping from behind the branches was Randy, Andy, The Smittens, and a few more from the lake. Except, they were not children any longer; they were grown-ups.

Raven wasted no time and jumped in the middle of the path. Her fingernails extended to sharp blades, and her fangs grew. She hunched as she hissed at the twins. She didn’t think about the outcome before she hurled herself at them. It was Andy that lifted his arms, and a swirling ball of air hit Raven in the middle of the chest, sending her plummeting to the ground.

“Stop, Andy!” Peggy yelled before joining Raven on the ground.

“She started it. Hissing at me like some snake.” He looked down at Raven. “I don’t mean you harm. We were under the control of Theo, and it limited our choices. We want Peggy back. That is all. There have been enough deaths already." He stepped closer, holding his hand out to Raven.

Her eyes roamed from one fairy to the other for a sign of evil. There was none. Minutes passed until she took the hand and felt her body pull to a stand. She gave a quick smile before returning to the Brandy Lee's side.

"Come here, Peggy. You are weak. You need us." Randy said, stretching his arms into a welcoming hug. A ribbon of lights of all colors jolted back and forth between his arms.

Peggy didn't hesitate. She ran into his arms. Rays of light circled the group as they all hugged. Peggy stood in the middle gleaming. Randy kissed the top of her head. She smiled. "I missed you." Raven and Brandy Lee watched. The love between the two was as loud as the wind. Peggy broke free then found her way back over to the girls.

She smiled from ear to ear before speaking. "I need to go with them. Please understand."

They smiled at their friend. Brandy Lee cupped the pure skin of her cheek. "We'll be fine. We're almost there, thanks to you. You need to be with your frollick. We'll miss you."

"Thank you, Peggy, for everything. We understand." Raven stepped in and hugged her close. "Can't say that I will not miss that magic of yours. It comes in handy."

"I'll miss you too. When you least expect it, I will be back." Peggy kissed both girls on their cheeks. "I hope you find your answers." She smiled. "Protect her, Raven," Peggy said before stepping back into her group. Randy wrapped his arms around her, and they turned into seven balls of rainbow lights. They lifted into the air and hovered for a movement. In one of the balls, Peggy's face appeared. Their eyes met one more time. A few tumbles in the air, and they whisked off upwards into the sky.

Raven and Brandy Lee stood there, watching the empty sky. They thought of how they would miss Peggy. Their hearts ripped between happiness and sadness for the fairy.

They turned to each other and kissed. "Let's put the tent up. We'll reach the council tomorrow. We need to rest. Brandy Lee leaned into her chest with her arms wrapping around her tiny waist.

Brandy Lee's words slipped out between sniffles. "I'll miss her."

"Me too." Raven held her tighter. "Me too."

23
Last Leg

The sun sat low on the horizon with the vibrant colors of rust painting the sky. Clouds so low, you could run a hand through the puffy white cotton. With the air thin, a breath was hard to catch. Roots, vines, and plants thickened as Brandy Lee and Raven traveled through the forest. The dense bush protected Raven from the dipping ball of fire, enabling the women to get an early start. Both wondered what Peggy was doing, but both felt happy that she was again with her frollick. Today was the day. They would reach the She-Wolf Council, thereby pleading their case that Brandy Lee was royalty. They could ask them to get the kill order removed, and then head back home to ordinary life. Well, as common as life could be. Raven's life could go back to serving as Queen Lana's assistant. Brandy Lee's life was still uncertain, but one thing was for sure. Raven wanted Brandy Lee in her life.

Raven reached back and helped Brandy Lee over a huge tree stump blocking their path. Just as Brandy Lee's foot lifted over the top, she toppled. They hit hard, knocking the wind out of them. As they sat up, they sucked in a small gasp of limited thin air.

"Damn that hurt. What happened?" Raven asked, wiping the mud off her knee. Her finger found a hole in her pants with her finger sticking through it. "Shit!" She said, wiggling her finger. She was on her last pair of shorts, finding that the council couldn't come fast enough. A hot, long bubble bath sounded so becoming. Brandy Lee's words ripped her from the short daydream.

"Something caught my foot." Brandy Lee jumped up and wiped the mud from her pants. Walking around Raven and placing both her arms under the armpits, she pulled her up. Brandy Lee brushed the sexy butt free from dirt. She shook her head to distract her from the cute derriere.

"I see you looking at my ass."

Brandy Lee smiled and wrapped her arms around Raven's stomach. Her chin rested on the back of her shoulder blade. With a deep content breath, she whispered, "It's a cute ass."

Raven laughed. She unraveled the arms wrapped around her and spun in one motion to face Brandy

Lee. Her arms laid on Brandy Lee's shoulders, with fingers interlocked behind her. "What have I created?"

"Hey, you created nothing that you can't handle." She placed a small kiss on the corner of her mouth. Brandy Lee felt the smile spread across Raven's face. There was a movement at the bottom of her feet, causing Brandy Lee to break the kiss and jerk her eyes earthward. Their shoes were barely visible through the jungle of brush at their feet. "It wasn't this thick a few minutes ago?"

Raven kicked one foot from the thicket and repeated with the other. Long claws extended to sharp weapons. With one swift strike, the vines cut into pieces, and Raven bent over pulling them away. Noticing the sexy ankle, Raven wrapped her fingers around it with the tip of her nails indenting the skin. Her fingers drifted the calf, teasing behind her knee. Small goosebumps peppered the flesh, and the leg shook. Raven smiled at the response. "You're shaking." She kissed the inner crease, letting her tongue trace a circular pattern. Raven's fingers feathered over her thigh. She slipped up her body spending a moment on the hard nipples. "You're still thinking about my cute ass?" Raven kissed her before Brandy Lee could answer. Their tongues swirled with moans releasing into each other. In the depths of a forest stood time. At that moment, it was only the two. Their pounding heartbeats synchronized.

Brandy Lee deepened the kiss. “Mmm…” Rolled from deep in her throat.

A sudden separation of their lips had them breathless. Their eyes widened, their pupils enlarging as both sets of feet pulled together. They grasped the other’s arm to stay upright. Their eyes fell as vines wrapped around the ankles, squeezing them together. They looked at each other in disbelief. A sharp stabbing pain hit them both, causing them both to grab at their necks. The world started to sway. A long dart protruded from each woman. Both dizzy with blurred vision, Brandy Lee and Raven tried to hold each other up in a stand. Something unseen yanked at their legs and they fell forward. They reached, desperately, with their hands before they were ripped apart and dragged into the forest. Names screamed in the darkness as they separated and disappeared underneath bushes.

24

Destination

"Ugh!" Her head was killing her. The tile under her body was cold and damp. Her face became indented by the texture of the floor. The air smelled like an old furnace. Brandy Lee pushed up on her arms, holding her weight with straight elbows. She shook her head. A pain seared through her temples. She peeked an eye open but then closed it. The slightest light filtering in the room hurt. She raised a hand and touched the bandage on the side of her neck. A dart? She remembered a dart sticking out of her neck. Raven? She had one too. Her eyes opened wide, and she searched the area as she ignored any radiating pain. It was a dungeon that caged her. Dull walls were moist from dampness. A tall ceiling with one window at the top was unreachable. The sun was out with rays streaking the walls fifty feet above into kaleidoscope forms.

She ran over to the solid steel bars that held her. Brandy Lee stretched her neck to the last millimeter. Her eyes roamed down the candlelit passage. She twisted and looked down the other way. A shadow passed at the end of the room. Brandy Lee watched as it paused for a moment, and in thought, she continued traveling.

"Hey! Where am I? I see you. Don't ignore me. Where's the other woman?" Brandy Lee's words fell on death ears. The shadow evaporated into a mist. "Damn it. Someone needs to answer me."

"Screaming will do you no good." The older voice came from the cell next to hers.

"Who are you? What is this place?" Brandy Lee wrapped her fingers around the bars, her face pressed against them.

"Me? Oh, I am a lost soul. A wolf that will never see the daylight of these dungeons' walls. My name is Agatha."

"What's your name?" The woman's voice asked.

"Brandy Lee. Where are we?"

"You're in the lovely accommodations of The She-Wolf Council. Your hostess is Alpha Victoria, along with her many deltas and betas. They serve dinner at six; lights out at seven in the evening.

The pacing started, and her breathing became ragged. Panic started to set over her. Why was she locked up, and where was Raven? The thought of Raven burning again – or worse – caused her heart to skip a beat. She grabbed the bars again, but this time for support. She bent at the waist, trying to suck the air into her lungs. She was changing.

"That won't do any good." The older woman's voice grabbed her attention. "Changing, that is. The bars are too strong, and it will just weaken you. If you're worried about that woman that came in with you, they dragged her down the end of the hallway and into the cells."

Brandy Lee took a breath. "Was she okay?"

"She was unconscious; appeared drugged. She's a vampire, isn't she?"

"Yes. She helped me find this place. The sun is up, and I am worried about her."

"Those cells don't have any windows, so the sun wouldn't be able to reach her. Why in the world would you want to come here?"

"Looking for answers." That was all the information Brandy Lee would disclose. Agatha seemed nice, but since they left the lake, Brandy Lee found it hard to trust. "Why are you here? Locked up?"

"Well, I got caught with my hand in the cookie jar." The older woman answered. "Been here, I think thirty years. I'm not sure. It could be longer. Time seems to stop in this hell hole."

"Thirty years? Jesus. That's a long time for theft.

What'd you try to steal? The royal jewels?"

Agatha's laughed echoed off the hollow walls. "Oh, lord! I haven't laughed like that in years. I haven't had a conversation with anyone other than the betas in thirty years, and they have no personality. You're refreshing."

"Good to hear, I guess. But that still doesn't explain why Alpha Victoria sentenced you to do thirty years for stealing something."

"I am not a thief, my dear. I got caught with my hand inside Cookie's jar. The mate's name of Alpha Victoria was Cookie. Understand now?"

"What?" The lightbulb lit up in Brandy Lee's brain. "Oh! Oh! You have been down here this long for that?" Brandy Lee asked.

"Alpha holds a grudge. Here is better than the punishment Cookie received. That gorgeous woman has been missing for three decades. She disappeared off the face of the earth. Supposedly, her body got thrown in the quicksand pit."

Brandy Lee slumped down against the wall. She remained quiet for a few minutes as she looked up at the window. It was hard to be sure, but it appeared there was close to two more hours of sunlight. Her heart was breaking, thinking of Raven alone surrounded by the prison's dark walls. Talking to Agatha helped with her anxiety, but Raven didn't have anyone. Brandy Lee rubbed her temples. A headache lingered in the background, and she needed to use the bathroom. Her eyes traveled over to the dark hole. *Nope! Not going to happen!* She thought. To take her mind off the screaming bladder, Brandy Lee went over her words that she would say in front of the council. They had to listen to her, and with the thought, a sigh released.

"What's the matter? Well, other than the obvious." Agatha questioned.

"I was thinking of my friend, the one they captured with me. She shouldn't be here. She should be home and in her mansion with Queen Lana. Not tramping around a forest with evil and not being burned alive. She should not be held as a prisoner in a dark dungeon." Brandy Lee ran at the solid bars and shook them. "Hey! Someone let me talk to Alpha. Now!" She screamed, anger filling her voice. Tears flowed down her cheek.

"I told you that would not help. No one can hear you. They'll get you when they are ready. Not before."

"Ah! I'm so frustrated."

Brandy Lee leaned her head back, closing her eyes. The sound of heels clicking down the blocks of stone caused her eyes to open wide. The closer the footsteps got, the louder the toe-to-heel beat ricocheted off the walls. Appearing in front of the bars was a tall, thin woman with short brown hair. Her eyes were the color of the blue sea. She wore a long red dress slit up to her thigh. Brandy Lee's eyes lowered to admire the nine-inch heels. The woman held a tray of food. She glared at Brandy Lee with endurance, demanding obedience.

Beauty of nature. Brandy Lee lowered her eyes and dipped her head in respect. She knew her status did not reach this woman's level in the pack. A beta wolf, she held her pose with confidence and power.

"Are you going to bite me, like your companion did when I handed her a glass of blood? If so, I would be glad to turn into my wolf form and remind you who I am. You can call me Beta Nichole."

"No, Beta Nichole. I won't try to bite you. I need to see Alpha Victoria, please." Brandy Lee's pleas were ignored; although, it was worth a shot.

"Our Alpha will see you when she is ready. Tell me, what's your name?" Nichole barked the question.

"My name's Brandy Lee, and…"

Her sentence ceased midway by a raised hand. "Stop. I don't care why you are here or how. I serve my Alpha; that's all. Whether you live or die does not matter to me. Now, take this platter from me." Another ordered barked.

Brandy Lee swallowed her pride and took the tray with closed lips. A fight to the death would be useless. "Thank you, Beta Nichole."

Nichole nodded and turned on her nine-inch heels. The clicking noise continued down the passageway. The faint clicking sound, along with

Brandy Lee's hopes, whispered away. She set the tray down on the floor and slumped back down against the wall. "What's she like? The Alpha?" She asked Agatha.

"Powerful; beautiful; determined. Loyal to her followers, but she will take your head off without hesitation if needed. You need to eat. I have a feeling you will need your strength. Oh, and the food sucks here."

Brandy Lee rubbed her eyes. A long night was ahead of her.

25
Alpha

Beta Nichole arrived two hours later with wolves by her side. She remained in her human form, but her companions appeared as she-wolves. They were small in stature, but with lean muscles and demanding power. Nichole leaned against the bars with one shoulder and her eyes falling to the half-eaten plate. “Glad to see you ate.” Nichole’s long red nails wrapped around the bars. The curve-hugging dress captured Brandy Lee’s eyes. “You like what you see?”

The question caught Brandy Lee off guard, and she weighed her answer. How could she not admire such beauty? “You’re gorgeous, but I’m with someone.”

Nichole huffed at the answer the young she-wolf

gave. "Alpha wants to see you. You need to wash yourselves. So," Her words stopped. Nichole turned her back to Brandy Lee and swayed over to the two wolves sitting in waiting. Her hand ran over their heads, giving a deep rub. "So, my friends will watch you take a bath. Oh, and don't take their petite size as a weakness. They'll rip you apart."

Brandy Lee stood there, glaring at the three. "And the other lady that you captured?" One eyebrow raised in question.

"You'll see her soon," Nichole answered the question with annoyance. Magically, an oversized copper key appeared. Nichole sauntered over to the steel door. The key slipped into the lock, and with a turn, a loud clang rang out. Nichole stared at her. "Can I expect trouble out of you?"

Brandy Lee lowered her eyes. "No, Beta Nichole. I know my place."

"Good." With a hard pull, the rusted metal door slid across the floor. The two wolves stood.

Brandy Lee stepped from her cell, and the brown wolves flanked her. She turned her head to glance at Agatha, who stood at her bars, watching. She was an older woman with long gray hair. Her brown eyes circled in wrinkles, gleaming at the sight of Brandy Lee. She smiled with a nod before a slow turn retreated her back into the cell.

A nudge at her lower leg pushed Brandy Lee forward. As they walked, she took notice of the tall stone walls. The castle's architect was magnificent. They entered a large room with two old-fashioned tubs, constructed of white marble with cast iron legs sitting in the middle of the floor. Steam swirled above the water with the aroma of lavender lingering in the air. Brandy Lee stopped in her tracks. Another nudge came from behind. Her eyes dropped to the sound of a snarl from one wolf. Teeth clenched. Brandy Lee took it as a warning and started to undress.

The warmth covered her body as she lowered into the tub. Two guards circled the tub before finding a resting place on the ground. Brandy Lee started to wash. She stopped when the door to the room opened, and two more wolves entered. Following them was Nichole and Raven in shackles.

"Raven." Brandy Lee pushed herself from the water, but a quick leap from a wolf and a sturdy snap of her jaws had Brandy Lee falling back. The water from the tub splashed out, wetting the wolf. She snapped again in the air and lowered down, shaking her head from side to side, causing a water spray. A growled released in frustration.

"Brandy Lee, stay put," Nichole yelled from across the room. She turned her head towards Raven, whose anger was apparent by the tight jawline. "I will undo these shackles. You'll get into the tub and bathe. When the two of you finish, we'll go to Alpha Victoria. If you try anything, and I mean any little thing, my four friends will rip your limbs from your body. Then and only then will they tear your head off, which will end your suffering. Do you understand?"

Raven's eyes stared straight ahead, but her head nodded. Once freed, Raven undressed and lowered into the water. Face to face in the tub, the lines in Raven's face relaxed.

"Are you okay? Have they hurt you?" Brandy Lee asked.

"No. I'm fine. And you?" Raven responded.

"I'm okay. Do as they ask. We'll see Alpha soon." Brandy Lee turned her head from one side of the room to the other. The four wolves laid around them at the four points of a compass. She noticed Nichole had left the room. "Wash yourself. They're watching us." Brandy Lee said. Both ladies picked up the wash clothes.

"Are you ready to see the Alpha?" Raven asked.

"I think so. A little scared." Brandy Lee whispered.

"You'll do fine. Remember to breathe." Raven responded.

The four lying wolves stood. The two small ones turned and walked into separate corners of the room. They soon returned with gym bags. Dropping them on the hard tile, the smallest one growled. *Dress!*

"She just told us to get dressed." Raven stood.

Her eyes met Brandy Lee. “Come on. And yes, I can still hear a wolf’s thoughts.” Raven said in an octave lower than a whisper to avoid her words from being heard.

The two women dressed in khaki pants and tee-shirts, slipping new sneakers over their feet. It felt good to have clean clothes. The fresh smell of lavender lingered over their skin and hair. Bodies so close, like a magnet they embraced and fell into a passionate kiss. The four wolves closed at the four corners. One paw over the other, they inched closer to the couple. A growl emerged. A door slammed open, stopping the wolves a mere moment away from pouncing. Their kiss broke, and they twisted around to find Nichole standing close.

“Enough. Let’s go!” Nichole spun on her heels. That dress so tight that it left no room for a misstep. Brandy Lee and Raven fell into the step with her, and the four wolves followed. As paws tipped over the stone, the four wolves changed into young girls. They appeared in their early twenties and fresh out of college. Everyone fell into a march. “If you’re wondering why they changed? You can’t be in your wolf form unless the Alpha is in hers.”

Entering by an enormous door, Brandy Lee and Raven started the walk of a thousand steps towards the throne. The path lined with women holding torches. Raven's eyes moved from side to side, admiring the elegance in the room. A mixture of hair color, skin tones, sizes, and shapes were displayed with power and strength.

Raven couldn't help thinking she wished she was wearing her Fitbit. All these steps were lost from counting. She laughed out loud at her thoughts, causing Brandy Lee and Nichole to flip a stare her way. She smiled. "Sorry." She whispered.

Arriving a short distance from the massive throne, hands placed on their shoulders pushed them to kneel. Brandy Lee grunted, and Raven hissed at the demand to lower. They were kneeling in front of three large chairs made of stone. The armrest on each chair carved into wolf heads. The eyes made of ruby jewels gleamed in the light. Shadows danced on the walls as torches flickered. The atmosphere was intimating, demanding, and dominant.

A thunderous noise ricocheted off the walls as the line women slammed the end of the torches to the ground. Straightening their backs with chins held high, their eagle eyes focused straight ahead. The side door opened.

The first lady to enter wore a long black dress that flowed behind her. Her solid gray hair white as snow touched the floor. Her nails painted in the color of midnight. The dress pushed up at the toe as she stepped with elegance across the floor. She sat in the first chair to the left. Both hands came to a rest on top of the carved wolf's head, her index finger rubbing between the wolf's eyes in long strokes. The eyes appeared to squint with pleasure.

The second lady's pace was much faster, and she was younger with spiked jet-black hair; a free spirit. A tight red short red dress painted her body like a canvas. When she took her seat at the first seat to the right, it hiked up so far, the crevice of her mound exposed for pleasure. A moment flashed, and she crossed her long legs, knee over knee. The sinful temptation tucked away.

"All lower!" The unison order bellowed from the two women.

Brandy Lee whispered. "Lower your eyes, Raven."

The room became silent as long clicking heels echoed off the hollow walls. Heel to toe repeated in long slow strides. Time froze. Breaths held.

Voices commanded. "You may raise your eyes!"

Brandy Lee and Raven lifted their chin in slow motion. Positioned in front of them was Alpha Victoria. A pure white cloth covered her body, a shoulder exposed. Her hair, the color of golden straw, rested mid-back. Her shoulders squared and a straight back; she sat with her ankles crossed. Unadulterated confidence radiated. She raked her nine-inch nail over her bottom lip, before leaning forward in her chair with both arms resting on the stone. She studied the two in front of her. The Alpha gave each the same admiration. Her head tilted from side to side: her eyes, the mixture of blue and gray, bore into their souls.

"I'm Alpha Victoria." She motioned right to the lady in black. "This is Delta Anne, and my third in command, the exquisite, Delta Monique." Her other hand swayed towards the lady in red. "And you're Brandy Lee. I received notice from Lady Rochelle that you were dead. How odd to see you alive in front of me. And very odd that you brought a vampire into our lair." Victoria leaned back in a slouch. "Why are you here? Speak," The order so powerful, Brandy Lee shivered.

A clearing of her throat and Brandy Lee stumbled the words out. "I don't know why the council heard that I was dead. That is not the case. But someone wants me dead. The vampires. They have put out an order to kill on me."

"A kill order? And yet one sits beside you?" Victoria asked.

"It was . . ." Raven spoke only two words.

"Were you told to speak? Quiet!" The words were ordered by Delta Anne. She sat on the edge of her seat. Raven lowered her eyes and clenched her fist.

"She helped me through the forest. It is a group of rogue vampires that have made attempts on my life, not the vampire council. At least, we hope not."

With a deep breath, a finger ran over her bottom lip again. Her speech paused for a moment before continuing. "You have traveled here to get the council to stop a kill order? It seems a little extreme." She said as she stood. The other two councilwomen stood up with her. Then, with swift movements, they descended towards them. "Stand, Brandy Lee." The other two women stood in front of Raven, towering over her.

She stood, but Alpha Victoria's power broadcasted in waves causing Brandy Lee to submit. "Fear. I smell fear on you." Victoria nudged her face into Brandy Lee's neck. She sniffed. Brandy Lee coward down. Victoria wrapped her arms around her waist and held her steady. She pushed the hair back from her neck, exposing the sleek curves. She licked from her collar bone up to the pulse of her neck. A small nibble and Victoria released a sexy growl. "You're gorgeous."

With a leap, Raven was ready to tear Victoria apart. A force pushed her back in one sweep. Delta Monique and Delta Anne stood to watch over her. Their teeth were glistening and low growls emerging from deep inside of them. "Stay down or die!"

Lips found Brandy Lee and took her into a deep kiss. Her hand grasped at her breast and palmed it. Brandy Lee melted into her.

Raven shook in anger to her core but held her spot. There were too many for her to kill, even though the death of the one clawing her girlfriend would satisfy enough.

"Lady Rochelle got word to me about your blood. I am in doubt. The royal family has not been in reign for centuries, but I will appease and play along with the game. If you are not of royal blood, I expect repayment for my time." She twisted the nipple in a gentle touch. Brandy Lee moaned. "Oh, you enjoyed that. Let me smell you." Her teeth sunk into Brandy Lee's neck. Blood filled her mouth. With wide eyes, she pulled back. "True, but not true. Taste," She orders her second and third in command. The two Deltas licked from the puncture with longing.

"She is not pure. I taste something." Delta Anne stated.

"Vampire. You have vampire blood." Alpha Victoria spoke. "Take them out of here. Get this abnormality away." Victoria turned and walked away.

Brandy Lee took a step in a desperate maneuver with pleas filling her voice. "There's no way that I have vampire blood. You taste the royalty. My reveal paper turned pure blue at my outing."

Sitting back on her throne, the Alpha was disturbed at the possibility. The thought of a living hybrid was uncharted waters. "You must die." She waved her hand in dismissal. Delta Anne and Delta Monique stepped towards her. Raven jumped in front of Brandy Lee to protect her.

"No, She must not. She is your royalty, and I

will explain the mixture of blood." The matured woman's voice so deep and seductive it danced around the walls. The words stopped everyone in their place.

"Empress Katherine, this is none of your concern. You can collect your vampire and leave us on our own."

"Oh, but it is Alpha Victoria. Brandy Lee is my daughter."

26
Mother

Radiating.

She drew all eyes towards her as long legs floated her toward Alpha Victoria. Not the first meeting of the two, so the visit was not unusual. The two councils' housing extends miles from each, often crossing paths since the treaty for peace got signed. Her curves, accented by the black pantsuit, clung to her body. The white shirt opened just above her belly button, revealing the soft space between her breasts. Her blonde hair bounced off her shoulders with each step. A black panther intensified her statue as the beautiful animal walked beside her with each stride — the beauty of nature.

Reaching the throne and standing a few feet from Brandy Lee and Raven, she dipped her head regarding the Alpha and her Deltas. “Alpha Victoria, please. Let me explain.” Empress Katherine, the highest of vampire empire, stood and waited for permission to speak.

“You have piqued my curiosity. Why did you call Brandy Lee your daughter? Please continue, but first,” Victoria looked around to place more emphasis on her next words. “Do you see any animals in my lair? Tell your companion to shape-shift or tell her to leave.” The powerful words flowed from her mouth.

Katherine's eyes shifted to the majestic cat that stood with her. She ran her hand from the back of her neck to her back. A purr vibrated off the walls. “Kachina, I need you to shift.”

Brandy Lee and Raven stood with jaws dropped since Katherine walked in the door. Raven in awe of the beauty of her leader. Her heart pounded against her rib cage as she stood frozen, a star-struck teenager. Brandy Lee remained in shock. She knew the words coming from Empress Katherine was a lie. Katherine couldn’t be a mother, especially her mother. Vampires could not have children, and the thought of the highest vampire being a she-wolf’s mother was ridiculous. The mere possibility circled inside her brain, causing her to be dizzy.

The majestic cat extended her body before limbs and jaws contorted. Olive skin replaced the black fur. The face surrounding the onyx eyes became human. She straightened her back before coming up on two legs. A Native American Indian woman of grace held her ground solid. Her jet-black hair cascaded the back like a waterfall. The high cheekbones enhanced the thin line lips. She wore a breechclout and moccasins that wrapped her body up in tradition.

"Thank you, Kachina." She turned her attention back to Victoria and the court, but not before matching Brandy Lee, glare for glare. They have the same golden eyes. She held the gaze when she spoke the next few words. "She's my daughter."

Her eyes shifted to Raven. Katherine cupped her face, the touch sending renewed electricity through Raven's body. "My child of the tribe. You are beautiful."

Raven turned her face into the touch, her eyes closed. With a quick drop, Raven kneeled at the feet of her empress. Words failed Raven. She felt a single finger raise her by the chin to a stand. "Stand with me, Raven." Raven slipped on the other side of Katherine, but her heart remained with Brandy Lee, who stood alone.

"You have our attention, Katherine. Tell us. What validates this claim of yours?" Victoria sat on the edge of her chair, waiting for logic. Delta Anne and Delta Monique mirrored her in their cathedra.

Katherine drew in a deep breath. A slight squint of her eyes, with wrinkles lifting around the edges, she looked at Brandy Lee without a falter. “While I was carrying Brandy Lee, a vampire attacked me. I should’ve died that night. You should’ve died.” Her stare focused on Brandy Lee as the words tumbled out. “I went into labor and gave birth to you in an alley. My body changing by the second, I had to do what was best. The vampire nicked your belly when she cut me with her claws.”

Brandy Lee ran her finger over her stomach. *The scar.*

“I left you at a firehouse, figuring the firemen would kill you if you changed. It was the hardest thing that I ever did. My insides died that day, but not from the vampire bite.” Katherine stepped closer to Brandy Lee. “Because I lost my baby girl.”

Brandy Lee wiped at a single tear that fell on her cheek. Katherine wiped at her own.

“I assume the wolf DNA that you carried in your body suppressed the vampire blood. I have watched you become a young, powerful woman. So,” Her words stopped. She turned and stepped towards Victoria. “She has a small amount of vampire blood running through her veins, but it’s she-wolf royalty blood that runs through her heart.”

Victoria sat in thought for a moment before speaking. “So? Who is trying to kill your daughter, and why?”

“Queen Lana informed me it was rogue vampires. They announced that Brandy Lee died while in the dark forest to reroute any attempts. It was a smart move because loose lips exposed the ones that wanted her dead. The possibility that a royal family member could turn back time, back to when war ravished the earth between our kind, scared them. We've taken care of them. Shall I say they have seen the light?"

Victoria leaned over, whispering into Anne and Monique's ear. The two women rose, leaving the room. They motioned Nichole to follow them. Victoria remained in her seat with a hard decision ahead of her. She didn't doubt that Katherine was telling the truth, but the question was what to do. The council was not ready to handle a hybrid, and neither was the world. But, if Brandy Lee was born as a member of the royal family, that news needed to get addressed. She took in a breath before reveling her decision.

"Brandy Lee will prove her heritage through two tests. If she is a royal family then, I, Alpha Victoria, will bow to our new leader. But, if not, you will be imprisoned for life." The entire room acknowledged with small howls.

Brandy Lee shuffled her feet in place. *Test! What test?* She opened her mouth to speak, but no words emerged. She was overwhelmed. Her biological mother, who tossed her away as a baby, stood nearby. Her blood carries vampire DNA, even though that is most likely the reason Raven healed.

That was one of the better thoughts in her head. Now, she must pass a test. Brandy Lee sighed. Being of the royal family meant nothing to her. All she wanted was to be back in her small apartment with Raven. If she refused to take the test, she would always be on the run or kept a prisoner. She swallowed before the words formed in her mouth. Just as she uttered the first syllable, the side door opened. Anne, Monique, Nichole, and a fourth body walked into the room.

Covered in a dark cloak that hid her identity, the strange woman got ushered to the center of the room. Forced to kneel, she sat quietly. Brandy Lee watched from a distance but turned her head when Alpha Victoria spoke. Delta Anne and Delta Monique flanked her once more.

"The first test. A fight." Victoria's words stopped by enormous cheers sounding off the walls. She lifted her hand to quiet the crowd. "Now, I don't approve of wolves killing their own. Unlike the vampires that seem to have no problem with it." Victoria gave Katherine a smirk. "So, if death occurs, then so be it. But…" Her eyes fell to Brandy Lee. "I better see one of you get hurt."

Victoria raised her body to a stand and motioned Nichole, who, with one hand, pulled Brandy Lee to the center of the room. She stopped in front of the cowering body beneath her. Brandy Lee jerked her arm away and spun to face Victoria. Rage painted the young girl's face. "I'll not fight." Brandy Lee screamed.

"Then to the dungeon you will go." Victoria lifted her head. Her eyes closed, and her body's shape started to shift. Her head jerked, and she landed on fours. Muscles defined with powerful, razor-sharp teeth clenched. The sleek curves of her back hypnotizing, she was the perfect she-wolf — the almighty.

Turning in slow circular motions, Brandy Lee watch the wolves appear. Bodies twisted and turned until they became their true selves. One gray and one black wolf soon sat beside Victoria on the throne. The Deltas were as impressive as the leader. Nichole growled after her change. She maneuvered Raven, Katherine, and Kachina into the corner of the room. The black panther appeared as they got pushed back away from the fight. There was an interchange of growls between the cat and the wolf. Kachina backed down. Nichole stood guard.

Raven took a step towards Brandy Lee. A grab around the wrist pulled her back. "She has to do this. I know you love her, but they outnumber us. Remain ever so still, my child." Katherine's words were soft.

Surrounded by hundreds of wolves, Brandy Lee felt more alone than she ever had. She glared at the cloaked woman and watched as shaking hands pulled the hood down off her head. Brandy Lee gasped. “Agatha?”

“It is okay, Brandy Lee. If you kill me, please make it fast. A slow death feels unfair after being imprisoned for thirty years.” Agatha stood, removing the cloth that wrapped her.

“I won’t kill you.” Brandy Lee said.

“Then you better hurt me, because this has to happen.” Agatha stepped back and shifted into an older wolf. Her fur was dirty; eyes sunken into the face. A weak growl emerged, revealing yellow teeth with some missing. She reared back and lurched towards Brandy Lee.

The hit tumbled them over, and the two rolled across the floor with Brandy Lee landing on top. Her body started to shift. Muscles formed, her canines growing from the extended jaw as she straddled Agatha. The white wolf tilted her head back and howled.

A piercing pain jolted her head downward. Agatha’s teeth pierced her right leg. The older wolf shook her head back and forth with a vengeance, tearing the flesh. Brandy Lee’s teeth dug into Agatha’s side, causing her to release the bite. They separated with both in a fight stance. A paw over paw dance commenced. They circled before the attack. Both ladies stood on their hind legs, small bites tearing the skin with claws ripping the flesh. Brandy Lee’s fur turned redder with each strike.

During one of the circling matches, Brandy Lee's

eyes caught Raven in the corner. The fear and anger covering her face broke Brandy Lee's heart. *Raven, can you hear me?* Brandy Lee thought.

Yes, I can. What can I do?

Can Victoria hear this? Brandy Lee asked just as she jumped away from a snap near her throat.

No, mind conversations are private between the wolf and me. Watch out! Raven yelled in her thoughts.

The dagger nails dug into the rib cage, and the lung punctured. Brandy Lee stumbled sideways. Her head shook, as she landed hard on her side. The air gone from her, she gasped. Agatha prepared for the final blow.

Brandy Lee, get up. Get up! Blind her with her blood. Now! In thought, Raven's words sounding desperate.

Brandy Lee jumped up and dug her teeth deep into the flesh above Agatha's eyes. Blood poured, blinding the older wolf. She backed up while shaking her head. A stumble, and she went down. Brandy Lee limped over with one collapsed lung. Breathing was difficult. She hovered over Agatha, her paw resting on her side. The older woman whimpered in pain from the head bite. Her eyes glued closed by her blood.

Brandy Lee's eyes searched the room before falling to rest on the throne of wolves. Time stood still between her and Victoria. With a final nod from Victoria, she ended the test. Brandy Lee turned and took a few steps towards Raven before collapsing. Raven joined her on the floor, pulling the wolf into her arms.

Victoria shifted back to her human form. She waited as everyone in the room followed. "The first test passed. Take our guests to their rooms for the night. The second test will be tomorrow evening. Katherine, are you staying?"

"I'll stay." The Empress answered.

"Nichole, make sure Empress Katherine gets placed in the best quarters. Give Agatha medical care and place her back in her cell. Feed her steak tonight, an award for her fight."

Delta Anne stood along with Delta Monique. The announcement came in unison. "All eyes lowered."

Alpha Victoria exited.

27

Love

Remaining in her wolf form, Brandy Lee laid gasping for air on the bed with breaths coming sparingly. Her side sunk in; evidence that the lung collapsed. White fur hardly visible through the bloodstains. Little whines emerged from the broken wolf.

"I can fix her!" Katherine said.

"No, she can heal herself. It'll hurt less." Raven responded. She wasted no time and grabbed Brandy Lee's backpack. Raven found the yellow vial of blood. She broke it into her mouth. As the blood of her sisters flowed through her veins, the rapid healing started. Her breaths returned, and wounds healed. Soon, Brandy Lee was sitting. Her breathing became normal. Raven rubbed her head. *You look better? Ready to change back?*

Brandy Lee gave a nod that was not reassuring. She wasn't ready to face the woman that claimed to be her mother. Standing in silence, while listening to her words and excuses spill out to Alpha Victoria, was torture. Brandy Lee closed her eyes. *I will never forgive her for giving me up,* she thought.

Hey! It'll be okay. I'll be here by your side. Always. Raven's thoughts sent in response.

Brandy Lee's eyes opened to find Raven smiling at her. She forgot Raven was listening. A hand touched the side of her face, and Brandy Lee turned into the palm. The face drew in, as the fur turned to the skin. The same palm now held Brandy Lee's cheek. She wobbled and felt the strong arms of Raven wrap her up into a hold. The covers pulled over her naked body. She sunk into the protection. After moments of gathering herself, Raven helped Brandy Lee to the shower. Blood and tears washed from her body.

Walking from the bathroom, Katherine and Kachina were still sitting in the room. Brandy Lee waved a finger at Kachina. "You helped us in the forest. With the kids, the snakes, Theo, and you helped us choose the right path. That was you. The panther."

Raven chimed in. "You dragged me through the woods when I got burned."

With hands folded in front of her, she nodded. A smile spread across her face. Her eyes asked Katherine to tell her story. Katherine rubbed her hand over the back of Kachina's head. "She lost her ability to talk when she was a child. Trolls cut her tongue out, and when I found her in the woods, she was close to death. I raised her as my own. She followed you because I asked. Queen Lana contacted me, telling me the two of you were traveling through the forest in an attempt to reach the She-Wolf Council. I figured the extra help would be worthy."

Kachina tapped Katherine grabbing her attention. Her hands started to move in odd movements. She was talking to Katherine in sign language. Both Brandy Lee and Raven studied sign language in school, but the speed that Kachina spoke was too fast to keep up.

"She says you make a cute couple, but some of your choices in the woods were dumb."

The two girls laughed. "We agree with you. We made very dumb choices. Thank you for your help. Both of us owe you our lives." Raven said.

"Can I ask you something, Kachina?" Brandy Lee stepped closer to her.

The Native American Indian nodded in approval. She leaned forward to listen to the question.

"When you change from panther to human, how do you keep clothes on your body? I am so tired of being nude after my change." Brandy Lee whispered as if she just said something dirty.

Kachina silently belly laughed. After a few moments, she walked over, leaning on the desk in the corner. A pen in hand, she started to scribble on a yellow pad. When she finished, she walked over to Brandy and handed the piece of paper to her. Eyes in the room watched as Brandy Lee read the article. A smile crossed her face.

"That's all?" Brandy Lee wrinkled her nose. "Really?" Brandy Lee said in astonishment at what she just read. Kachina's head moved up and down. "All this time, I was naked, and this was all I had to do? Wow, I feel stupid. Thank you."

Kachina signed welcome.

The room got quiet long enough for Brandy Lee's thoughts to go wonky. She looked around the room. They were in a room with no windows, and one noticeable king-size bed. They were in her and Raven's place, and the adrenaline pumping through her veins caused her mind to drift into a vision of what could come later. The first time they would make love in a bed. Sex in a tent might be something she wants to revisit one day. Although, she wanted Raven here, making love in this bed.

"Can we talk privately, Brandy Lee?" Katherine asked. The words ripped her back into reality. She released an inner moan for the interruption.

Her eyes found her girlfriend. Without words,

Raven told her it was okay. "Sure." Brandy Lee answered with zero enthusiasm.

She felt the kiss on her cheek. "I need to look for blood." Raven said.

"Kachina, take Raven to our room. You'll find bags of blood there. Help yourself."

"Thank you, Empress. I'll be back in fifteen minutes." Another kiss lingered on the cheek of her lover. Raven left followed by Kachina.

The young she-wolf sat beside the woman, claiming to be her mother. Her hands twisted around each other in a nervous habit. Over her entire life, she dreamed of the words she would say if this day ever became true. Words filled with love, rainbows, sunshine, and others ending with hate, storms, and choice words. She sat, unable to catch her breath with no words forming. It was Katherine that spoke first.

"I don't expect forgiveness. But I'm glad that I could tell you the story. I did what was . . ." Katherine's words got cut.

"What was best for me? I heard that part. I grew up in shitty foster homes because of you. At eighteen, I couldn't wait to get away from the houses of no love. I was a paycheck to my foster parents. Oh, I know there are foster parents out there that do good, but I never had one of them. You hid Kachina. Why couldn't you hide me?"

"Kachina was already a shapeshifter when I

found her, and that was after I took the throne. I couldn't risk other vampires killing you. I fought my way to the highest seat. They didn't hand it to me. If I had a human baby on the streets, they would've killed you."

The tears started to flow down Brandy Lee's cheek. She tried to hold back her emotions, but they overwhelmed her. "I look like you." She blurted out.

"You also look like your father. You have his lips and temperament. He was a police officer. We were so young. He loved you. He always sang to my belly, hoping you heard him. We went to the movies that night. I insisted we take a shortcut back to our apartment. The vampire attacked us in the dark alley. Your father's death was instant, and my attack was much slower. The slow pace of the kill had a crowd come towards my screams for help. Before they arrived, the vampires ran. And, so did I. The change started. They would have killed you and me. I ran a block over, and you started to arrive." Katherine inhaled. "You know the rest."

"What was my name? The name you and my father chose?"

Katherine smiled. She paused for a moment in thought before whispering the name off her lips, "Lavonne Ann."

Brandy Lee bit her lower lip, a strategy she learned as a young child to stop tears from flowing.

"It's a nice name. I don't know what to expect from this." Her hand waved back and forth between herself and Katherine.

"Expect nothing. Pass the test tomorrow and worry about the next day later. Prove that royal blood runs through your heart. And afterward, if there's a tiny space in that heart for me, we'll find it."

A knock on the door startled both women. Raven popped her head in the door. "Can I come in?"

"Yes, I'm just leaving." Katherine leaned over and placed a kiss on Brandy Lee's cheek. "Thank you for listening to me." She walked beside Raven on her way out. She stopped, placing a hand on her shoulder. "Watch after her. She loves you. See the two of you in the morning." Katherine opened the door and turned before she slipped out. "You turned yourself into an amazing woman." She whispered before closing the door behind her.

Brandy Lee watched as Raven fell to her knees and leaned into her. With arms wrapped around each other, they held each other close. A few minutes slipped by, and Brandy Lee felt the body in her arms lift with heaves. Sobs muffled by a hug. They laid in the dark, holding each other tight. No words. No sex. Unspoken love.

28
Pillow Talk

The red numbers on the clock glowed in the darkness. The only light in the room was an eyesore that Raven kept peeking at with one eye. She dozed for an hour before her body woke, only to repeat it over again. Brandy Lee lay next to her sound asleep. The fight was exhausting, and sleep came quickly, as soon as she closed her eyes. Raven's mind wandered in a mountain of fret. A few hours ago, her emotions surfaced, and she broke. The fear of losing Brandy Lee was too much to handle. She'd fallen in love with her, an unusual sentiment for Raven. She loved in the past, but nothing compared to the feeling she'd developed for the cute blonde next to her. The thought of losing her tomorrow was eating at her insides. Raven stirred and fell to her back with an arm covering her eyes. *From where were these emotions coming, and why*

couldn't I stop crying? The pillow moistened with her tears. She sniffled too loud, and Brandy Lee rolled into her. Raven wrapped her free arm around the woman and drew the warm body closer. She watched as she snuggled into her — a perfect fit.

"Baby! You're crying again?" Brandy Lee whispered out in the dark.

Raven froze. The thought of Brandy Lee worrying about her was the last thing she wanted. But then, she never wanted to lie to her either. "Just a little. I was thinking of you and this test tomorrow. My mind is too busy, and I can't sleep. That stupid clock is driving me crazy."

"What time is it?" Brandy Lee asked.

"A little after one. Six more hours till nightfall. Go back to sleep and get your rest."

Raven felt a finger circling her belly button along with a tingle rising. She suppressed her moan. A single touch and this woman unraveled her. Her touch was the most addicting drug.

"I would rather pillow talk." Brandy Lee growled her words.

"I like pillow talk." The answer came between a hitch of breath.

Fingers teased their way into the band of her pajamas, and Raven sucked in her belly as a response. Her skin was on fire from anticipation, but when the fingers stopped at the top of her mound, a moan of disappointment escaped. "Don't stop," Raven begged, the plea for touch denied as the hand withdrew. Raven pumped her hips, searching for the fingers. She felt Brandy's body slip on top of her, and every nerve ending fired up. Their mouths invaded each other with tongues dancing. Raven's hands roamed her body like a map. Every curve and crevice touched with grasping fingers. "If you don't take these clothes off, I'll rip them off."

"Then, you strip too." Brandy Lee whispered as she snaked her way down.

Raven wasted no time following the request. With her butt raised, she yanked and twisted until she laid naked from the waist down in the bed. Brandy Lee took her top and bottoms off in a tease. The removing of her clothing was slow and sensual, causing Raven to bite her lower lip until she tasted a tinge of salty blood. Her body was beautiful, and Raven could not hide her desires.

Brandy Lee raised an eyebrow in question. A tilt of the head and her eyes pointed to the top that remained on Raven. With arms crossed, she waved a finger towards the pajama top in a request for removal.

"Oh, sorry." Raven sat up and with great haste, slipping the top off before tossing it to the floor. She laid back down, exposed.

"Much better." Brandy Lee whispered.

When lips kissed the inside of her thighs, Raven

shivered with electrifying chills. She couldn't remember the last time a woman tasted her. She rarely allowed it. A mouth on her was like the last link of a chain. The sexual act was personal, and Raven wasn't one to give it away freely. But she would allow it tonight with this woman. She could think of nothing else other than that mouth sucking her clit — the mere thought bringing her to the edge. A soft kiss in the crevice of her hip and the word screamed from her mouth on its own. "Stop." Raven felt the pull away, and then the withdraw. She saw the confusion and hurt in her eyes. "I'm sorry. I didn't mean to scare you. It's just . . ." Her words trailed off. She covered her eyes with her arm. The next thing she felt was Brandy Lee straddling her stomach, the coolness of her vagina chilling her skin. A hand wrapped around her wrist, followed by an arm pull.

"What's the matter?" Brandy Lee asked.

"I'm sorry."

"Yes, you already said that. Tell me what is going on." Brandy Lee asked, her face becoming lit by the only light in the room and that annoying clock.

Raven inhaled. Her fingers circled Brandy Lee's thigh, causing goosebumps to appear. She loved that her touch affected her in that manner. "I haven't had a woman's mouth on me in a very long time. Only two women have ever tasted me."

"I don't have to do that if you don't want me to. I should've asked."

"No. That's not it." Raven inhaled, then exhaled. "All I can think about is your mouth on me. I was about to come."

"Oh, I see. So, you worry about coming too soon." Brandy Lee was on all fours hovering over Raven.

"Yes," Raven whispered, her voice huskier than before because of the sexy creature's body poised above her.

"I want two minutes." The words whispered just above Raven's lips. "I'll place my mouth on you, and you'll not come before two minutes passes. You've watched that clock all night, so it's time to watch it again. When the clock clicks past the two minutes, give all of you to me. Let me taste your juices. Come."

The words caused a puddle to form in Raven's center. Two minutes would seem like a lifetime, therefore it was a promise she could not make. She nodded in response. She couldn't concentrate on speaking; breathing was her current priority. This woman was taking her to an unknown ledge. A moan rang out as the nipple got sucked in hard; the teasing a shortcoming as Brandy Lee moved to the position between her legs. A yank at the knees and her legs spread apart with ease. The center hidden by soft curls. She watched as Brandy Lee's tongue ran over her bottom lip in hunger. For a moment, their eyes met before finding the clock. They waited with nerves on edge for the number to change.

With a flip of the digit, Brandy Lee smiled. "Aww…Two minutes."

She felt fingers spread her wide. A tongue rolled over her center. "Fuck," She bucked. *Concentrate on the clock. Damn clock.* Her heart pounded, and breaths became ragged. Her clit throbbed for release. But, not yet. Her hips started to thrust but halted when her clit got sucked in with passion. "Slower, I can't make it." Raven begged. It was the first time that she ever solicited a woman to go slower.

A long sigh of relief released as the clit slipped loose. "One minute!" Raven cried out as swirls around her folds had her building. Her eyes fell away from the clock and she watched the blonde hair bob between her. "Oh, god!" The orgasm was building. She needed to last thirty more seconds. She gritted her teeth in desperation.

When a tongue slithered inside of her and tickled the inner walls, Raven grasped the head between her legs. "Jesus! What're you doing?" Raven asked, but no answer followed. In and out with the speed building faster and faster. The wake was starting. Hips thrust wildly up and down in rhythm. The tongue dipped deep inside, curled and ran over her soft spot at the same moment the clock clicked a digit.

"Two minutes!" Raven screamed as she released. Waves of orgasm flooded her body as she gave every bit of herself to Brandy Lee.

Soaked between her legs, tender at a mere touch; Raven collapsed into the bed with after climax moans filling the air. She watched as Brandy Lee crawled her way back up. So sexy. One swift roll, and she was on top. The wetness found between her legs pleased Raven. "Kiss me." Raven ordered as she slipped two fingers in her.

A moan breathed into the kiss was the reward, and Raven took her. Her fingers moved in and out with her thumb, rolling over a swollen clit. Her body pressed her down onto the bed. Raven wrapped her fingers up in the blonde hair, giving a little yank, as it exposed the sleek curve of her neck.

"Yes; please," Brandy Lee pleaded.

Her fangs dug just below the surface, and she drank from her love. The motion of her fingers slipped to the edge and then dove deep back inside after fired excitement. She felt her own climax topping again. Brandy Lee bucked wildly under her in pleasure. Feeling the woman beneath her tighten as she drove her fingers deeper and sucked with fury. Brandy Lee screamed in ecstasy under her as walls clasped around her fingers, and she exploded. Raven followed with her second.

"I like pillow talk," Raven admitted. "I even like

that stupid red clock."

Brandy Lee stirred in after sex, half-asleep and intoxicated. "I love you."

"I love you too."

Wrapped in each other arms, both drifted off.

29
Test Two

The elevator dinged as they reached their rooftop destination. The doors separated with a breeze swirling into the box, lifting the women's hair. They stepped from the elevator, with the full moon greeting them along with lounge chairs, tables, and umbrellas. Victoria sat at one of the patio tables, enjoying an assortment of breakfast dishes with a cup of coffee. Behind her, Anne and Monique relaxed in the lounge chairs sipping on mimosas.

"Welcome, ladies. Come grab a bite to eat." Victoria waved her hand over the table.

The three women found a seat with Kachina, grabbing a plate before joining the Deltas.

Brandy Lee's plate filled within seconds of sitting. As her fork dug into eggs, followed by a mouth full of bacon shoved in before the first swallow, her cheeks puffed out. "Sorry, I eat a lot."

The words mumbled from a full mouth. She pointed the fork at Raven. “She can tell you.”

Raven shrugged her shoulders at Katherine. “I think it is a she-wolf thing.”

A relaxed laugh emerged from Victoria, a rarely seen occasion. “I assure you I have a hearty appetite, but nothing that compares to that.”

“How are you feeling, Brandy Lee?” Victoria asked.

“I feel good. Nervous. Ready for this to be all behind me.”

“What is the test, Victoria? Let’s get this over with.” Katherine said with a snap in her words.

“Now, Katherine, your quarters were not up to your standards. You seem grumpy.” Victoria joked.

“You damn well know that is not the case.” Victoria snapped back.

“Sorry, fine.” Victoria stood, grabbing her coffee cup. She strolled over to the wall and looked out into the forest, glancing at nature’s beauty with evil lurking within. She motioned the other women to join her. “Can you see that patch of green to the north?”

Brandy Lee followed the tip of Victoria’s finger to a flat area a mile away. The trees had been removed, and a few lights flickered in the distance in a cleared area. She squinted, trying to make out the small items on the ground. Tombstones? The stones were erected in a linear formation, contrasted the blackness that surrounded them. “A cemetery.”

“Not just any cemetery. The royal family cemetery.” Victoria turned and leaned on the wall. “Inside the cemetery lies the last family member to die, and she’s wearing the family jewel — a blue sapphire necklace. If you’re of the royal family, you’ll be able to remove the necklace from her neck. If you are not of royal blood, your body will turn to gray ash when the jewel gets touched. Call it the perfect DNA test. Return with the necklace around your neck and claim your spot; or, die out there.” Victoria turned her head, allowing her eyes to search the horizon.

“I am going with her!” Raven blurted.

Victoria twisted her mouth in thought. “Suit yourself. I would stay away from the jewels, though.”

“Kachina,” Katherine yelled for the Native American woman to join her.

“No.” Victoria held her hand, stopping Kachina in her approach. “Only one can go with her to the royal cemetery. That’s all that I will allow. Choose one only.”

“Brandy Lee, please let Kachina accompany you,” Katherine said.

“It will be Raven. She’s been by my side the entire time. End of discussion.” Brandy Lee's words held firm. “Let’s go. I’m ready to be over with this.”

“Wait!” Katherine spouted. She inhaled when everyone stopped to listen. “Victoria, the mixture in her blood may get her killed.”

“Well, Empress Katherine, just as that wolf blood saved her from turning the first time, let's hope it saves her again. I have spoken and will accept nothing less than a proof of her heritage.” Victoria swayed away from the ladies. At a snap of her fingers, Anne and Monique followed her off the rooftop. She turned before entering the elevator. “I hope that I see you again, Brandy Lee. I have grown fond of you.” A few steps and the elevator door closed behind her, leaving the four visitors alone.

Brandy Lee looked up at the moon and raised her chin to the fully round figure high in the air. “I’m ready. It’s time.” Her eyes fell to Katherine. “I’m not sure what to say. Goodbye, mother.” The name didn’t come easy, but Brandy Lee wanted to say it at least once in her life. She turned to Kachina while saying the words. “Goodbye, my friend.” She acknowledged with a smile.

Raven and Brandy Lee stepped away from the wall’s security and made their way to the forest’s edge. They stood in front of the towering trees with backpacks around their shoulders and determination in their hearts. Brandy Lee reached down, grabbing Raven's hand.

"Here we go again," Brandy Lee said with a smile.

The vines grew thick, and the path lost. Once more, Brandy Lee stopped and wiped the sweat off her forehead. She downed a bottle of water in one gulp. "Damn, it's hot!" She said before wiping another layer of sweat off her head.

"It's a little warm. At least, we don't have far to go." Raven responded. She sat down on a fallen tree and patted next to her for Brandy Lee to sit. "We can stop for a minute." They opened another bottle of water and shared it.

Something fell from the tree and hit the ground behind them. Twisting at the waist, Brandy Lee and Raven saw nothing. An apple rolled between their legs into the open space, coming to a stop a foot away. Another one fell and tumbled towards them, stopping by Raven's foot.

"What the hell?" Raven jumped up and spun around, looking for the source behind the rolling apples. A red one fell, hitting Raven on the shoulder. "Shit! That hurt." There was laughter.

Brandy Lee joined her, and the two women stood back to back. "Who's that laughing?" Brandy Lee asked. "Please, tell me it is not children." When the next apple hit at their feet, Brandy Lee picked it up and threw it back into the treetops. Something or someone threw it back at her. There was more laughter. “Let’s leave, Raven.”

The words were barely out of her mouth before the monkey fell from the trees, landing on Brandy Lee’s back. Screaming and circling, she grabbed at the monkey. The animal was laughing and slapping at her while riding her.

Raven reached to pull it off her back when one jumped on her arm and shuffled to the top of her head. A yank and she tossed him to the ground. “Mother Fucker!” She yelled as she grabbed the one on Brandy Lee’s back and tossed it to the ground.

They both ran at them, kicking the dirt in their direction. The girls froze in their tracks when ten more monkeys emerged from the brush. They laughed, showing sharp yellow teeth, as they stood on two legs banging at their chest. Teeth clattered in monkey talk while paws scraped the dirt like a bull waiting to attack.

“We need to move, now,” Brandy Lee screamed. They didn’t look back. They sprinted into the forest at high speed. The leaves from the treetops toppled down on them as they got chased from above.

A clearing was ahead. “Head to that field.” Brandy Lee screamed. Coming to a sudden halt in the middle of a circular field, they searched for the animals. The surrounding trees were silent. Something scared them. Maybe, Katherine sent

Kachina and went against Victoria's demands. No, Katherine wouldn't have jeopardized the aftermath between the two councils by ignoring Victoria's rules. The reason their chasers fled didn't matter now. They were gone.

Both ladies placed their hands on their knees, breaths labored. "They disappeared," Raven said as she looked around. "And it looks like we are off course."

"That wasn't any fun." Brandy Lee went to take a step, and she sank into the ground. She tried to lift her other foot, but it disappeared deeper. "Raven, I'm sinking."

The step Raven took towards Brandy Lee was a failed attempt. Her foot sunk to the ankle. She twisted her upper body, scanning the area. The field was a perfect circle. Turning the other direction caused her body to dig deeper into the ground. They were in quicksand. "Don't move, Brandy Lee. We're in quicksand."

Sunken to their waist, and scared, the situation seemed hopeless. There was nothing on which they could grab or pull. The panic started to set in, and Brandy Lee was feeling anxiety toward consuming her. Breaths were coming harder, and she was fighting the change. Her wolf weight was more substantial than the human form, so remaining a human was vital.

"What're we going to do?" Brandy Lee's eyes

filled with tears.

"I don't know. There is nothing around us." Raven was having breathing problems as the quicksand crushed her chest.

"I'm so sorry. Please, forgive me." Brandy Lee pleaded for forgiveness. "If it weren't for me, you wouldn't be here." She began to shake, which sunk her faster.

"Calm down. I love you."

"I love you too."

The thick liquid lingered at their chin. With chins titled towards the moon in desperation, they fought to the last minute. They gulped the last frantic breaths before the earth swallowed them.

Death wasn't too bad. No pain. She felt her body lifting upwards. She must be on the path to heaven with an angel carrying her to the other world, but there was no light. Where was this light about which people spoke? It was dark. Brandy Lee tried to open her eyes, but they were heavy. Continuing upwards, relenting to the unknown, she broke the surface. The weight lifted from her eyelids, and she blinked at a rapid pace.

She barely spoke the name. "Peggy?" She collapsed in the arms of the fairy. To her right, Raven's body surfaced and fell into the waiting arms of Andy. In a fireman's carry by Peggy and Andy, the two women's bodies maneuvered over a tree, bridging the way to solid ground. Randy stood with arms stretch outward and palms up, holding the trees sturdy over the quicksand. Collapsing to the ground, the women rolled to their side in a coughing fit. Brandy Lee raised upon straightening arms just in time to see two trees swallowed up by the earth.

"Hi, ladies," Peggy's cheerful voice rang out. The tone of her voice sounded like a greeting for a casual meeting between friends. Not like she just pulled her two friends from death's door. "You two look a mess."

Brandy Lee fell back in laughter while reaching over and giving Raven's thigh a loving squeeze. Her hand pushed back the quicksand that caked hair back away from her face. The sticky goo was drying like cement on her. She turned her head to look at Raven who remained on her side. "You hurt?"

"No, just scared." She responded. "You?"

"Same." Brandy Lee answered. Turning her head, she found Peggy in Randy's arms. They made a cute couple. "Can we get one of those showers again?" Brandy Lee asked.

Peggy smiled. "No problem, my friend."

30
Family Jewels

Raven and Brandy Lee sat across from Peggy, Randy, and Andy, smiling at their friends. The Smittens and the other fairies guarded the perimeter against the monkeys. They attacked them for the last hour before retreating into the woods, not to return. Peggy made a shower for the two women, pulling natural ingredients from the forest to make soap and shampoo. All signs of the struggle for life disappeared from their bodies.

"Thank you. We are grateful to you," Raven said.

"I agree. Thank you. You saved our lives." Brandy Lee added.

"Ladies, you saved us back at the lake. One good turn deserves another. We were in the right place at the right time." Randy answered for the group. His arm wrapped around Peggy, protecting his love.

"He is right, you know. I would still be Pigpen Peggy, if not for you two. And Andy would still be an asshole." The five of them laughed. Andy shrugged his shoulders. "We'll help you get to the cemetery. With all of us together, we have the strength to fly you there. We can't go inside, however; the aurora of sadness that lurks around the sacred ground will kill us. But we will wait for you outside and fly you back to the castle."

Raven nodded. "So, how do we do this? Fly there?" Raven asked.

"Just stand still and hold on." Peggy smiled with the words.

"Hold on? To what?" Raven asked with skepticism.

Peggy sang out a note so powerful; the leaves fell from trembling trees. The fairies flew over, and streaks of rainbow lit the sky. They twirled around, dancing above Raven and Brandy Lee's heads. The mixtures of the colors and love cocooned the two women. They were inside a ball and lifting into the air, giggling as they tumbled head over heel. Their arms pushed against the walls for balance. The colors blended, and laughter rang out. The fairies were laughing. Were they floating? No, they were flying. Less than five minutes later, Raven and Brandy Lee felt their feet hit the ground. The ball disappeared into the night. A single strand of rainbow flickered in front of them. Inside the bright colors of red, orange, blue, and greens floated Peggy. Her wings fluttered, as she hovered.

"We'll be here waiting for you. Good luck, my friends." The streak flew off into the night.

The girls turned on their heels to face the rusted iron gate in front of them. Both swallowed the knots forming in the back of their throats. The gate door broke and hung to one side. A crow, perched on the spikes that protruded from the top of the black metal, flapped her wings. "Caw! Caw!" She screeched. A warning? But, for who?

Raven took a step back, and Brandy Lee grabbed her hand, steadying her. "I hate birds," Raven admitted. As if feeling her fear, the bird flapped her wings and flew above Raven's head. The wind from her wings whisked over her skin. "Fuck!" Raven fell backward. Her arms swatted over her head in a frantic state, causing her to hit the ground. "No! No!" Her body curled into the fetal position.

"Hey, it's okay. The bird is gone." Brandy Lee used every assuring word of which she could think in order to soothe the terrified girl. She pulled her into an embrace and felt the shaking of her body as she held her close. "I promise I'll protect you."

"I am sorry. My fear of birds is crippling." Raven was calming at a slow pace in her arms. She could stand after a few minutes. Her eyes focused back on the gate, and her hands brushed the dirt off her pants. A deep breath with a slow exhale, and she gathered her composure. This show of heroism was not one of her more elegant moments.

She and Brandy Lee stepped forward past the gate. The girl's eyes scanned around while they stepped deeper into the graveyard. Hundreds of tombstones lined the ground. Some were plain, and some elegantly carved with pictures, but everyone held the royal crest. The ground sunk in areas, while a few leaned sideways. Dead oak trees filled in the spaces between the graves.

"So, how do we find your relative that has the jewel?" Raven asked.

"We're looking for the grave of Sissy MacKamzie." The small giggle from Raven drew her eyes away from the tombstone; she was reading. "What's funny?" Brandy Lee followed the question with a chuckle.

"That name does not sound like a big bad she-wolf royal family member."

Brandy Lee laughed out loud. "I guess not." Her eyes scanned row after row of graves. "There are too many to search through. Let's split up."

"I don't like that idea. We should stay together." Raven responded.

"Look, you go down that row, and I will do this one. We are one row over and can see each other." Brandy Lee threw the solution out to Raven's concern. It seemed to work because Raven moved one row over. She started to stroll while reading the names of the dead.

"Is the ground squishy to you?" Raven asked as she jumped in place.

"Don't even go there." Brandy Lee's response came with a sudden halt in her steps. "Raven." When there was no answer, Brandy Lee repeated the name louder. "Raven."

"What?" Raven turned. "Oh! You found it." She jumped over one grave to get to where Brandy Lee stood fixated on the tombstone.

"I can't get the jewel. There's no way that I'm going to dig up a child." Brandy Lee announced just as Raven arrived at her side.

"What're you talking about, a child?"

"Look at the dates." Brady Lee pointed at the tombstone.

Etched in gray two-tone stone, the weathered worn name appeared.

Sissy MacKamzie
Born: 11/9/1109
Died: 10/31/1119

"She was ten years old and died on Halloween. I am not digging up a child. Let's go." Brandy Lee started to walk. She stopped and turned when Raven didn't follow. Turning back around, she found

Raven squatting next to the grave marker, reading it carefully. "Come on, Raven. Forget it."

"Come. Look at this." Raven motioned with her hand for Brandy Lee to come back over to the stone. Brushing at the rough texture, small pieces of mud fell to the ground.

"Stop that." Brandy Lee fussed as she ran back towards Raven.

"Will you just look, woman?" Raven rubbed at the second number in the death date. The one turned to a seven in front of their eyes. "She died in 1719, making her 610 years old. She wasn't a child when she died. Now, how do we get the jewel?"

Brandy Lee leaned over and inspected the numbers. Raven was right. Dirt had covered the numbers. "We have to dig the grave up and open the coffin. After that, I have to remove the necklace off her neck all while hoping I don't turn into ash."

Raven coughed. "You said open the coffin?"

"Yes." Brandy Lee raised an eyebrow. "You are not afraid? I thought coffins were a vampire's thing?" Brandy Lee received a look of aggravation which she ignored. "Step back and let me show you my superpower." A jerk of the head and she jumped in the air, landing on all fours. Her head shook from side to side while she snapped at the air. A small step and she hovered over the grave. Her front paws clawed and dug, tossing the dirt into a massive mound between her back legs. The ground opened under her at a rapid speed. After digging close to six feet below the ground, she sat back on her behind, releasing a sneeze. *I hate it when dirt gets up my nose,* she thought. Brandy Lee was sitting on a coffin. She looked up at the paler than regular face of Raven. *What?*

"Um…nothing. You just enjoyed that a little too much."

Who doesn't like to dig a hole? It's fun, she thought.

"I'll just take your word for it," Raven said. Raven jumped into the hole just as Brandy Lee changed back to human. "Let's get the necklace and get the hell out of here."

Both ladies stepped beside the coffin. Taking a moment, they inhaled. They pushed with their shoulders, and the lid creaked as it lifted. There was a loud click when the coffin lid opened to the fullest. Once it came to a rest in its final position, the women stepped back and stared inside.

Sissy laid there dressed in the traditional white wrap. Her arms rested crisscrossed on her chest. She looked asleep, in peace. Wrapped around her neck was a large gold chain and sitting in the center of her chest was a blue sapphire jewel. When the moon hit the stone, a light the color of the ocean circled the dirt walls inside of the grave.

A single tear fell. Brandy Lee wiped at it. She nervously bit at her lower lip, rotating in the small space between the coffin and dirt wall to face Raven. "If I turn into ash, know that I love you. Get back home and enjoy your life."

"Stop with that talk. You are royalty, and nothing will happen. I love you, and my plan is going home with you. We will enjoy our life." Raven pulled her closer. Her lips brushed over hers before deepening. Neither woman wanted to pull away but found the strength to withdraw at the same time. Their foreheads lingered and pressed together for a moment.

With a shuffle, Brandy Lee was looking over Sissy, wondering how they were related. Maybe a cousin, grandparent, or perhaps an aunt. She inhaled and reached out with trembling fingers. She withdrew her hand, lowering her head. A touch on her shoulder built her confidence, and she reached out with her fingers wrapping around the blue sapphire. A bright beam of light shot between her fingers and lit the sky above them, reaching the moon. Brandy Lee's body jerked. Her eyes rolled back into her head. She stiffened and cried out before collapsing on the corpse. Muscles quaked in convulsions, and the air filled with the aroma of burning hair. Flames shot between her fingers as her grasp on the blue jewel tightened.

Raven stood lost with her hand over her mouth and nose. The smell was terrible, and she was close to gagging. If she pulled her away, everything they went through would be for nothing. But she couldn't sit and watch her die. Just as she reached out to touch her, Brandy Lee straightened. She screamed and yanked the jewel. The necklace broke off in her hand. The blue light dimmed, and Raven's eyes widened. Brandy Lee turned towards her. She was out of breath but breathing. Shaken but standing. In her hands dangled the necklace, as she held it tight. For the second time tonight, Raven's jaw dropped.

"What's the matter?" Brandy Lee's voice shook when she talked. The words slipped out between heavy breaths. "I did it. Why are you looking at me?"

"Your hair." Raven spit the words out. Her finger pointed to the blonde mane.

"My hair?" Brandy Lee asked. She had leaned back against the coffin for support.

"You have a black ash streak running through your hair."

Brandy Lee pulled at the end of the hair. Mixed between the blonde strands were dark spots. She shook her head. "What the hell? Maybe the vampire blood caused my hair to turn to ash instead of me. My wolf blood protected me from burning."

"You did it! Put that necklace away so I can hug you."

Brandy Lee tossed the artifact in her front pocket and fell into her arms. She never felt so protected and in love. “Let’s bury Sissy back up and get the hell out of dodge.” Brandy Lee whispered into Raven’s chest.

31
The Proof

The yellow flowers that Brandy Lee found in the corner of the cemetery looked out of place on Sissy's tombstone. Placing them on the grave felt appropriate since the tomb got invaded moments earlier. Brandy Lee laid a hand on the top of the stone and lowered her head in thought. They never met, but she felt a connection to her.

A growl vibrated through the air, and Raven and Brandy Lee stilled. What in the hell could this be? It sounded large. Moments after filling in the dirt, Brandy Lee changed back to a human. By the time Raven turned towards her to see if she heard the noise, a wolf stood shoulder-length next to her. Brandy Lee turned her head slowly to meet Raven's face. *That is a hellhound growl. I need you to be ready to fight.*

Red eyes pierced the night behind a massive

headstone. The girls took note that there were three sets of demonic eyes staring at them. The dogs from hell traveled in packs of threes. White teeth clenched with upper lips curled in a snarl, penetrating the darkness. They crouched low to the ground, ready to attack.

Raven's fangs extended; her fingers grew into sharp weapons. Brandy Lee lowered in an attack formation. Low growls and hissing emerged from the two. Two of the hellhounds pounced at Brandy Lee. Catching the throat of one hound, she clamped down. Blood poured from the wound. Tossing the small scraggly dog to the ground, Brandy Lee attacked the second one. Their bodies flipped over and over.

The third hell hound attacked Raven from the side. One step and Raven wrapped her in a headlock. The hound snapped his jaws while attempting to latch onto flesh. Raven's claws dug into the side of the hellhound's throat, reaching her spine from the front. Raven tore her fingers across, opening a huge gap. The head flopped back, and the blood drained from the body. The dog went limp in Raven's arms before being tossed to the side. Raven's eyes searched and found Brandy Lee against a tombstone. She and the other animal snapped and clawed at each other with fiery, whimpers intertwining between growls.

The bite administered by Brandy Lee on the first

hound healed and the animal prepared to attack. The black dog leaned back, ready to launch when Raven jumped at her. She overshot the target and tumbled to the ground, knocking the hound off Brandy Lee. The hellhounds gathered themselves together, preparing for the second assault.

Raven, we need to get out of here. Get on my back. She spoke to Raven with her thoughts. Raven didn't question the request and jumped up on the large white wolf. She wrapped her fingers in the black fur that ran down the once pure white coat. Brandy Lee leaped into a run with the hellhounds following in chase.

The gate was a few hundred yards away. Raven turned her head, and in her vision, there was two black dogs with matted fur with foam dripping from their mouths. They chomped at the air as they grew closer. "Um…Brandy Lee. Pick up the pace!" Raven yelled over the wind.

Hold on! With a huge leap, their bodies flew over the gate, landing hard on the ground on the other side. Raven wobbled to the side but grasped at the fur to hold herself steady. The hellhounds stopped at the gate. Loud barks echoed as they attacked the cast-iron rods, but not passing through them. Brandy Lee and Raven turned to see the two hounds rotate in a few circles before jumping back into the graveyard.

Brandy Lee lowered, and Raven disembarked.

After she was on the ground, the wolf twisted, turning into the blonde woman. On her knees, her head held was low. The shapeshifting was making her tired. Looking down at her body, she had on clothes. She made a mental note to again thank Kachina for the lesson.

"Wow. You look like Cruella Deville." Peggy's voice approached.

"Funny." Brandy Lee fell onto her butt exhausted, but excited. She got the jewel and fought off monkeys and hellhounds. She needed to get back to the council to prove her heritage; then, they could go home. As if being heard, the fairies circled and lifted the two. Within minutes, they stood in the she-wolf royal court.

Alpha Victoria sat on her throne, studying the tired young blonde in front of her. She cocked her head, admiring the black strip of hair running from her hairline until it laid on her shoulders. Grabbing a piece of unknown meat from a bowl, Victoria dropped it in her mouth. Passing the bowl over to Delta Monique, she nodded to Brandy Lee. Monique stood, walking over and handing her the bowl. Taking the bowl, she nodded to the Delta. She needed to feed so she could gather her strength.

Devouring the meat, Brandy Lee wiped her mouth before turning to the court. A gold chain followed by a shining blue sapphire got pulled from her pocket. The three ladies of the court slid to the edge of their chairs, their eyes widening. Empress Katherine stepped from the corner to eye the stone. It was captivating. Brandy Lee spread the clasp apart, wrapping it around her neck. The blue stone laid perfectly above her heart.

Alpha Victoria rose. Her feet glided over the steps until she stood in front of Brandy Lee. The silence was deafening. Not a breath heard in the court. Victoria admired the necklace with a gleam before her eyes found the golden ones. Alpha Victoria dropped to her knees in front of Brandy Lee. The entire court followed.

Brandy Lee looked around in a daze. She zipped her lips together, and the words slipped from the corner of her mouth. "Alpha Victoria, what're you doing?" Brandy Lee whispered. "Get up, please."

"I am honoring your Highness." Victoria said.

Brandy Lee looked over at Raven, Katherine, Kachina, and Peggy, while shrugging her shoulders. She wasn't sure what to do. "Rise all!" She stated in a demanding tone. It worked because the entire room rose in a swift movement.

"We'll prepare your room and throne," Alpha Victoria said.

"No, I am going home to Lady Rochelle and

with Raven."

"Your Highness, your place is here as our royal family. The vampires may try to kill you again."

Katherine stepped forward. "That won't happen again. Once they know that she is my daughter, it would be suicide for a vampire to try."

"Your Highness, please," Victoria pleaded.

"Calling me Your Highness is weird. Stop it. Look, I want a simple life. Raven and I eating popcorn and watching movies." The two women took the time to send love messages with their eyes. "I am going home, and you run the council. All stays the same. No, wait. One thing changes. You will release Agatha."

"Yes. Your Hi . . ." Victoria bit her tongue. "Yes, Brandy Lee."

A tall, auburn-haired woman swayed across the room. Her eyes remained lowered as she stood in front of the newest royal family member with a lockbox. "What's this?" Brandy Lee asked.

"It is for the royal necklace. We'll keep it locked up in the vault. It is too dangerous to leave it out. We don't want anyone to turn to ash by accident."

"I see." The necklace was removed and locked away. She walked over and hugged Victoria. "You're doing a great job here. Continue. I will be in touch."

Brandy Lee joined her friends. She hugged Kachina. "Thank you for your help." She turned to

Katherine. “Please keep in contact. I would love to get to know you better.” She wrapped her arms around the Empress and held her for a moment. Hearts beat together. She was ready to go home. Tired and with the nightfall disappearing, she wanted to be with Raven in a bed in their hometown. “Can you get us home?” she asked Peggy.

“Yes, not a problem. I want you to know that you are a special friend to me.”

“And you to me.” Brandy Lee wrapped her up in a bear hug. The giggles from Peggy radiated between the two. She kissed her cheek before releasing her.

“Ready?” She held her hand out to Raven.

“So ready.” Their hands slapped together.

With a nod, the women got wrapped in a rainbow ball. It jiggled in the air before streaking into the moonlight. They were homebound.

32
Home & Heart

Brandy Lee and Raven leaned against the Lexus beside each other, watching the pedestrians hurry by in a rush. The streets were crowded and noisy this evening with a crisp fall air heavy on the skin. Humans and vampires walked down the street, smiling at the sexy women. She-wolves lowered their eyes with a dip of the head in respect as they passed by Brandy Lee. A few she-wolves' eyes widened at first glance of Her Royal Highness. Word spread fast around the world about a royal family member emerging to power. Only two weeks since returning home, it was impossible for Brandy Lee to go into public without a paparazzi frenzy. Being locked away with Raven was a plus for the socializing sacrifice. The message sent to Alpha Victoria and Lady Rochelle instructed the high seated she-wolves that Brandy Lee wished to remain behind the scenes and study under Rochelle. They were doing a great job controlling it all, and Brandy Lee didn't see any reason to rock the boat.

Raven slipped in front of Brandy Lee and pushed her against the car. She leaned over, kissing down her neck and nibbling over the pulse. "You look amazing tonight. I'd much rather take you home and remove this dress piece by piece until you stand in front of me in nothing but the purple lace underwear you are wearing."

Dressed in a long gown that hung to her body, and sheer material revealing skin that only teased the eyes, Brandy Lee looked fantastic tonight. Her beauty only accented by the woman in the black lace dress by her side. Brandy Lee wrapped her arms around her neck and pulled the woman she loved closer. Raven was unraveling her with her mouth. "You keep this up, and we will not make it to the ball."

At the first mention of the debutante ball for Brandy Lee, she declined the thought. Lady Rochelle talked her into it, using the excuse that her Pack deserved the chance to honor her. She caved into the request, but only if her friends would be there. Other than having this woman sucking on her neck, she was excited to see Peggy and the other fairies. Empress Katherine and Kachina are coming, along with Alpha Victoria and her court. Brandy Lee made sure Agatha got invited.

The door swung open to the high rise, and Raven pulled from Brandy Lee. A blush covered their face, as their idols stepped into the moonlight. Sisters Lady Rochelle and Queen Lana dressed in formal gowns, drawing the eyes of passersby. Brandy Lee and Raven stood straight up as they approached.

"Evening!" The two women said in unison.

Queen Lana stepped beside Raven and pulled her into a side hug, leaving her arm around the young girl's waist in a hold.

Lady Rochelle closed the space between her and Brandy Lee. She circled, an undertone growl whispering out as she rubbed her head into blonde hair. She sniffed. Brandy Lee stood still with breaths held and eyes forward. The mere touch of her mentor caused the young she-wolf to square her shoulders. A deep long vibrating growl resonated from the back of Brandy Lee's throat. Lady Rochelle smiled.

"Something's missing, Brandy Lee." Lady Rochelle whispered in her ear.

"What's that, Lady Rochelle?"

"Fear. I no longer smell fear on you."

Brandy Lee's smile spread from her mouth to her eyes. She turned and wrapped Lady Rochelle in a hug. "Good, then your teachings are a success." She said.

"You know you don't have to do this." Lady Rochelle's words caught Brandy Lee off guard. She pulled from the hug.

"Now you tell me I need not go the ball?"

"No, young one. You need to go to the ball. I am just saying you do not have to drive us to the ball. We just hired a new driver to replace the last one I had. She didn't work out. Had higher things to do with her life." Lady Rochelle smiled, as she shoulder nudged her.

Brandy Lee giggled. She jingled the car keys. "I love driving you. You take me on the most amazing adventures." Brandy Lee opened the door, allowing the sisters to get into the back seat.

She opened the front door for Raven and watched as the woman stopped short of dipping into the car. Brandy Lee took Raven's hand, placing it over her heart. She whispered. "As long as blood runs through my heart, I'll always love you."

The End

Thank you for reading ***Blood Runs Through The Heart.***

We always appreciate reviews.

If you enjoyed this book, please check out these amazing lesbian themed authors.

You can find our books on Amazon. Thanks for reading!

Lila Bruce
https://www.amazon.com/Lila-Bruce/e/B00O7XHJZ0?ref=sr_ntt_srch_lnk_2&qid=1571015978&sr=1-2

Lise Gold
https://www.amazon.com/Lise-Gold/e/B06XJTCWF8?ref=sr_ntt_srch_lnk_1&qid=1571015949&sr=1-1

KC Luck
https://www.amazon.com/KC-Luck/e/B07BK5ZRYT?ref=sr_ntt_srch_lnk_1&qid=1571015728&sr=1-1

T.B. Markinson
https://www.amazon.com/T-B-Markinson/e/B00DUR9B82?ref=sr_ntt_srch_lnk_1&qid=1571018237&sr=1-1

Ocean
https://www.amazon.com/Ocean/e/B01MFDXPYT?ref=sr_ntt_srch_lnk_1&qid=1571017185&sr=1-1

L L Shelton
https://www.amazon.com/L-L-Shelton/e/B07DTHCPS9?ref=sr_ntt_srch_lnk_1&qid=1571016081&sr=1-1

Thank you

For

Reading